BAD ATTITUDE

BAD ATTITUDE

WEREWITCH™ BOOK ONE

RENÉE JAGGÉR

LMBPN PUBLISHING

LMBPN Publishing
PMB 196, 2540 South Maryland Pkwy
Las Vegas, NV 89109

First US edition, February 2020
ebook ISBN: 978-1-64202-759-4
Print ISBN: 978-1-64202-760-0

CHAPTER ONE

If it wasn't for all the fights, the Bristling Elk would have been a nice, peaceful place. It was an old-time country and western bar combined with a family-owned diner, located off the main street leading through the center of Greenhearth, Oregon.

At about 10:30 in the morning on a weekday, the place wasn't exactly bustling with customers. No band played country tunes, no bodies moved to music. There were five people on the dance floor, though.

Four against one.

"Now," the apparent leader of the four young men began, "we *asked* you a simple question, is all." His name was Chris, and he was tall, although not much taller than the girl.

He took a step forward, pointing at her. Meanwhile, his buddies fanned out, two to his left and one to his right, the quartet of them penning the tall young woman in at the far corner of the floor.

She didn't move. All she did was stand, hands on hips,

glaring at them, her hazel eyes mostly lidded. The rest of her face was twisted into an expression not far from being a wry smirk. A hint of freckles dusted her nose, but they did nothing to make her look any less serious.

"Yeah," the girl shot back, "and I gave you an answer. Get out of my face, if you would, please. I got better things to do with my time than talk about dumbass crap like that."

The beefiest of the four laughed at that in a stunned, scoffing way, as if asking, "Can you believe this shit?"

Chris, the leader, seemed less amused. His face fell in dismay even as his eyes widened. "What the fuck?" he snapped, taking another step forward. "You got *no* cause to give us this kind of attitude, especially since we can't help being curious about…people like you. All we were doing was—"

He took another two steps forward, ignoring the way the girl had tensed up, raised her eyelids, and laser-focused on him as he'd made his first move.

She suddenly stepped forward, interposing her foot between his and shoving him hard in the chest with the side of her forearm at an angle. Before he realized what was happening, he was tumbling hard into the floor, his cowboy boots sticking up at the end of long, flailing legs.

Then his boys jumped in, and it was on. The handful of other patrons all turned to watch the show.

Just before the good stuff began, a young man wandered into the building, shaking the day's cool, misting rain from his shoulders and closing the door behind him with his foot.

He stood about six foot two and wore a fringed brown leather jacket and cowboy boots of his own. They were common footwear in the region. His hair was short but shaggy, his eyes bright and blue, and his square jaw was covered with beard stubble.

There was a notable resemblance between him and the girl on the dance floor. He looked to be about her age, or perhaps a year or two younger.

He made straight for the bar, not yet glancing toward the scene developing off to the side. Cheryl, the one waitress currently on duty, noticed him at once and strode toward him.

"Hi, Jacob," she greeted him, her eyes sparkling surreptitiously. "Aren't you just looking all sweaty and rugged today!"

He shook the moisture off his coat. "Just the rain," he chuckled, "but thanks, Cheryl. Not yet decided if I'm going to eat or not. Probably a beer will be enough."

"Gotcha," she acknowledged. "Up to you. Oh, I don't know if you noticed, but Bailey's picking a fight again." The waitress gestured at the dance floor with her elbow but kept her eyes on Jacob.

He looked past her shoulder, taking in the scene. The girl was only seconds away from throwing Chris on his ass.

"Well," he mused, rubbing his stubbly chin, "technically, it's four guys against her. Really, it seems more like them ganging up on Bailey than her 'picking a fight,' if you ask me."

Shrugging as Bailey stepped forward and launched Chris earthward with her sudden takedown, Jacob smiled and closed the rest of the distance to the bar. He plopped himself down on the nearest stool and flagged down the bartender.

"Two beers, please," he requested. Only one was for him. "Bailey's going to be thirsty after she gets done with her workout over there."

The bartender, a jowly man with a calm, friendly face, nodded and quickly produced the brews, the bottles lightly coated with frost and perspiration.

The bar area could be a watering hole in any American small town. It was dimly lit, but not to the point of obscuring the place. Signs and placards advertising different alcohol brands were attached to the walls, some of them with neon borders and logos.

Behind the bar were a few mounted photos of different iconic places in the Cascade Mountains—Mount Hood, Mount Jefferson, the South Sister—as well as the mounted head of an eight-point buck the proprietor had bagged during a deer-hunting trip into Idaho three years ago.

Jacob had always thought that an elk would have been more appropriate than a white-tail, given the name of the establishment, but the man hadn't gotten around to that yet.

All in all, the place had a definite "redneck" vibe, but more than that, visitors thought it felt homey.

"Damn," Jacob commented as he reclined, sipping his lager while watching the fight, "those guys actually aren't doing too bad."

None of them was down for the count, and they'd even landed a couple of minor, glancing blows on Bailey. They all looked just barely old enough to legally drink, so they were probably still learning how to hold their liquor without doing anything too stupid. Then again, some people *never* learned.

Bailey's foot caught Chris in the stomach. *"Oof!"* he sputtered, doubling over as his eyes bulged and his charge halted. The blow had killed his forward momentum.

One of the other guys had tried to grab the young lady from behind, wrapping a beefy arm around her shoulders, but she'd reached up, seized his ear, and pulled his head down by it just in time to jump straight up and kick his buddy.

With that taken care of, she rolled around to the side of the man attempting to grapple her and released his ear as she swept his legs out from under him with a strong lateral kick, shoving back and down on his chest for good measure. He toppled like a felled tree, landing flat on his back on the dance floor. The impact knocked the wind out of his lungs.

The other two had also been sprawled on the ground, but now they were climbing back to their feet.

Bailey settled into a combat stance, grinning with bared teeth as the pair of them moved in to try to flank her. Chris was regaining his composure, and his eyes were livid with rage. She put up her fists to welcome them.

About this time, the door opened again and two more young men strolled in. One was about the same height as Jacob and similar-looking, although he was thinner and slightly younger—probably in his late teens.

The other one bore a resemblance as well, but he was five or six inches taller—he had to be a good six foot seven—and darker in hair, complexion, and demeanor. Both caught sight of Jacob and walked up to join him at the bar.

The bartender reappeared. "Howdy, Kurt," he greeted

the younger, average-sized one. "And Russell." He nodded at the brooding, towering young man. "What'll it be?"

"Beer," Russell said in his deep, gravelly voice.

"Hmm," Kurt began, making a show of trying to decide, "a beer *does* sound good right about now, but for some reason, there's this 'law' that says I can't drink yet. So unless you'd be so kind as to slip me a brew without bothering with all that ID nonsense, well, I guess I'll have to ask for a Coke."

The bartender sighed. "One beer and one Coke, coming up." He turned to grab their beverages.

By now, all three were watching the fight, chuckling at each new swing of a fist, each stumble or curse, and each impact of a body on the floor. The four dipshits weren't having much luck defeating Bailey, but they refused to give up.

Returning with two bottles, one golden and one dark brown, the bartender asked, "She's not smashing up any of the equipment or furniture over there, is she?"

Kurt accepted his legal, non-alcoholic cola. "Nope. Denting the floorboards a little is all."

There were four other people, three guys and a girl, watching the brawl from closer to ground zero. One of them, a skinny straw-haired kid named Justin who lived on the other side of the valley, picked up his beer and retreated to the bar to sit next to the three brothers.

"Hey," he greeted them.

They all waved at him. Jacob realized he hadn't seen the kid here before. He must have just turned twenty-one recently.

Justin squinted at the trio beside him and then the fight

going on at the other end of the building. "What I don't get is why you guys aren't coming to the rescue? You're not going to let her get beaten up, are you?"

Kurt shrugged, and Russell didn't say or do anything. Jacob spoke for all three. "She's the oldest of us," he pointed out, "so she'd hand us our asses if we jumped in without being asked. Besides, looks like she's doing all right."

No sooner had he said this than subsequent events made him into a liar.

Chris and the skinniest of the four guys came at Bailey simultaneously from separate oblique angles, trying to seize her arms. While she was momentarily distracted, the biggest and beefiest of the four snuck up behind her with surprising stealth and took a swing. His fist caught her pretty hard on the cheekbone just in front of the ear.

"Ow!" she bellowed, head falling forward as her four attackers all laughed.

The big guy who'd hit her chortled. "How you like that, bitch? You've been lucky so far is all."

Jacob sat up straight. "Uh-oh." He swallowed about half of his beer in one gulp. Beside him, Kurt was wincing, and even Russell had lowered his eyes to the floor, subtle tension filling his huge frame.

On the dance floor, Bailey's eyes were positively blazing, and she trembled.

Motioning to the bartender, Jacob told him, "Mr. Quaile, you'd best call the cops. And an ambulance. Things are about to get ugly."

The man threw up his hands. "Oh, for God's sake!" He put down the glass he'd been polishing and hustled to the establishment's landline.

Justin raised an eyebrow, confused. "What's wrong? I mean, yeah, that was a decent hit, but she seems okay."

Jacob shook his head. "It's not that. She really doesn't like being called a 'bitch.' It's a family thing, you might say. Somebody's about to get seriously hurt."

The words had just left his mouth when Bailey spun toward the beefy asshole. Her fist was like a piston as it drove into his midsection with a speed and force that made her previous blows seem like something thrown in a light sparring match with a kid half her size.

The big guy's eyes bulged and his mouth dropped open. "Auulggh!" he squawked, and a sickening crunch was audible from his chest. He dropped to his knees, clutching the spot she'd punched him, and gasped in pain. He would no longer be participating in the fight. Jacob was sure of that.

The other three moved back in. They were motivated to get revenge now, but didn't seem to realize that Bailey had stopped treating this as a half-assed sporting fight and was now playing for keeps.

One of Chris's wingmen, the scrawniest of the four, reached her first. Her hand shot out in a fierce grasping motion, seizing him by his shaggy hair and jerking his head and upper body forward hard enough to make him squawk. Then she drove her knee into his gut, put her other hand on his shirt, and tossed him the full length of the dance floor.

He landed just before the wall and skidded into it head-first. His body shuddered from the jolt, and he was silent for a second before a series of low, miserable groans escaped him.

That left Chris and the nondescript fourth guy, who both piled on her, fists swinging wildly, knees and feet lashing out.

As Jacob watched, the waitress came back over to check on him. Or at least, that would be her official story; she probably just wanted to be near him and have an excuse to strike up a conversation.

He raised a hand to her. "I'm good, thanks."

"Okay," she responded. "So, did you come here often before I started working?"

Jacob smiled. "Ever since it was legal, so about two years now."

"Gotcha." She wasn't sure what to say next, so she wandered off, figuring she might have another opportunity later.

Back on the dance floor, Bailey had taken a couple more minor, glancing blows as the remaining two dipshits flailed madly at her. It looked like the fight would be over soon, though, and not in their favor.

The young woman swept Chris's left leg out from under him with her foot at the same time as she shoved his chest hard with both hands, sending him hopping and stumbling five or six feet back before he simply toppled over.

As this was going on, the fourth guy laid a hand on her shoulder, trying to reposition her so he could land a punch on her jaw. She was faster, though, both of her hands seizing his wrist and twisting it sharply.

He cried out and drew it back to his chest. That gave Bailey an opening to kick him in the gut, sending him to join his friends on the floor. He didn't get back up.

Chris wasn't down for the count yet, though. He'd fallen hard and was struggling to rise to his hands and knees. Bailey pounced on him, sitting on his lower back and grabbing the same ankle she'd just kicked out from under him.

"*Ow!* Fuck!" he exclaimed. Unlike his buddy's wrist, she twisted his leg slowly, not doing immediate serious damage but threatening far worse. The spectators winced as his foot began to pivot in a distinctly unnatural direction.

Bailey looked down at him. "Uncle?" she suggested.

"I, uh," he wheezed. "Uncle. *Fine.*" He tapped the floor rapidly with one hand.

The girl released him, leaving him trembling and breathing heavily as she sprang to her feet. "Right, then," she said. "Best gather up your low-IQ friends and get out of here once you get some air back in your lungs. Hope you *learned* something."

Watching, the three brothers chuckled darkly.

"Yeah," Kurt opined, "for their sake, I hope so, too."

Bailey's ears picked up the sirens growing louder and closer as she wandered over to the bar. She'd left her four victims behind, sprawled on the dance floor, to think things over.

Her three brothers were waiting for her there. They watched her with a mixture of cool admiration and concern for the consequences of what had just happened.

After she arrived, they glared at the quartet of dumbasses, bristling with hostility.

Jacob had an extra beer in his hand. "Here you go, Sis. Figured you could stand to get your mouth wet after all that."

"Thanks." She took it from him and placed it against her face, between the cheekbone and the hair, where the beefy guy's fist had landed.

Now that the adrenaline rush of combat was wearing off, the shiner was stinging her fiercely, and behind it was a deep ache that suggested bruising. She might even have some kind of fracture, though probably not. The cold glass soothed it quickly enough.

She sighed, wanting to drink but holding off for the moment.

"I can't *believe*," she complained to no one in particular, "that I managed to get sucker-punched. It's embarrassing is what it is."

Once her cheek was numb, she withdrew the bottle, snapped off the cap, and angled it almost straight up as she gulped the amber liquid, draining half of it before she came back up for air.

"Wow," Kurt marveled, exaggerating his look of wide-eyed wonder. "That stuff numbs pain from the outside *and* the inside! Being twenty-one must be the best thing ever."

Jacob prodded his shoulder. "Too bad it'll never happen for you, squirt."

"Yeah, yeah, shut up." Kurt savored the next drink of his cola as if it were fine wine.

The sirens grew blaringly loud as the vehicles producing

them pulled up into the diner's parking lot, then the noise cut off all at once. There were a few shuffling sounds and footsteps while everyone within waited for the inevitable.

Sure enough, the door burst open and in streamed the forces of law and order. Said forces were represented in this case by two cops in front, hands resting on their sidearms, followed closely by two paramedics. They quickly surveyed the scene.

Officer Jurgensen, who seemed to be in charge, let his gaze linger for a moment on the crumpled forms of the four guys on the dance floor. Then he shook his head, sighed, and waved for the others to follow him in that direction. They ignored everyone else in the bar.

Chris sat up, his jaw slack and his wide eyes not comprehending what he was seeing for a moment. Then he scootched forward and pointed at Bailey.

"Officer! Thank God you're here. That woman is responsible for all this. We asked her a simple question, and she started acting all hostile and stuff. My buddy got overexcited and called her a 'bitch,' and she went ballistic on us. Totally psycho. We're gonna need medical attention while you're arresting her."

Jurgensen stood before the young man with his hands on his hips, his bony face displaying a hint of sympathy but mostly annoyance.

"You're under arrest, my friends," he stated, "although you are entitled to medical attention as well. Don't you worry about that."

"What?" Chris protested as the two paramedics circled around the two cops to examine him and his friends.

Jurgensen by now had shifted his right hand to the

nightstick at his belt. "Go picking fights by calling her a 'bitch' again and I'll billy-club you myself."

Pouting as he slowly climbed to his feet and wincing from all the blows he'd taken, as well as his twisted ankle, Chris stammered, "But I thought you were protecting us! 'To protect and serve,' isn't that you guys' motto or something?"

"Yeah," said Jurgensen. His partner came up beside him. "That *is* protecting you, dumbass. You boys look familiar. If you're from around here, I would've thought you'd understand things in this town have a unique way of working. If you're knocked unconscious, you can't go around spewing stupid, troublemaking shit like that where her brothers will have to take notice."

All four of the defeated quartet were now fully conscious again and either sitting, kneeling, or standing. All their heads turned toward the other quartet at the bar.

Bailey was ignoring them, focused on her beer. Her brothers, though, were staring menacingly at the dance floor. Even the smallest of them was almost the same size as the beefy dude who'd punched Bailey on the cheek. The eyes of the huge towering one practically smoldered, as if he were fantasizing about murder and giving serious consideration to making his daydream a reality.

Those on the dance floor all looked at the floor or walls instead.

The paramedics finished their examinations and one of them stood up.

"Okay," he began, "two broken ribs on the big guy. Broken wrist on the skinny guy. The gentleman over there has a mild concussion, and this guy," he pointed at Chris, "doesn't have any major injuries we can identify, but we'd better look him over in more detail."

"Right," Jurgensen assented. "Do so."

The paramedics led the four battered ruffians out the front door, aside from the largest one with the busted ribs, whom they'd placed on a gurney. The other cop chaperoned the group while Officer Jurgensen hung back, then slowly strolled toward the bar and came to a halt beside Bailey.

"You, young lady," he intoned, "need to work on managing your anger. I'm getting pretty tired of these kinds of incidents."

Bailey puckered her lips out in a fake pout. "Aww, but Officer, this *is* how I manage it."

"Real cute," Jurgensen replied. "But see to it that you don't *manage* it into some kind of disaster that brings in the press or the outside authorities. I'm willing to overlook crap like this to a point out of respect for your family, and Sheriff Browne understands. It's another thing entirely if the State Police—or, God help us, the feds—get involved."

Kurt piped up. "Dang! I didn't know the FBI investigated bar brawls these days." He sipped his Coke. Jacob shot him a glance, not sure whether to smack him or burst out laughing.

"Watch it," Jurgensen grumbled, and strode out the front door without further words.

As he exited, he passed a woman coming in, a blonde in her early thirties or so—Tomi, the long-time waitress, who usually worked both lunch and dinner.

Tomi glanced around. "Damn, looks like I just missed

the excitement." Shaking her head, she went to get her apron.

Meanwhile, another of the handful of spectators, most of whom seemed disappointed that the fight was over already, wandered toward Bailey. He was a good old boy in his late twenties or so with an almost perfectly round goatee.

"Hey," he interjected, "you're Bailey Nordin, aren't you? You work at the body shop, right?"

The girl took another swig of beer. "Yeah, that's me," she confirmed. "Don't work there as much as I ought yet, though." She gestured behind her with a nod of her head. "And those three guys over there are my little brothers."

The guy waved at them but did not make eye contact for long. "They don't look all that little, but okay. Listen, I was thinking of doing some improvements on my truck."

Bailey perked up and gave the young man her full attention. "Oh, really? And what was your name again? Don't think you mentioned."

Her new friend smiled. "Chris. No relation to that other guy you just beat up, ha, don't worry. See, I was thinking my truck could stand to be lifted—you know, so it sits higher on the wheels—and maybe add a flame decal on the front. And an oil change."

"Really?" Bailey quipped. "Well, we could get you set up at the shop, or I can give you some tips on how to do it yourself, although it helps if you already know a few things about motor vehicle repair and improvement."

The Nordin brothers watched as Bailey regaled the guy with a virtual encyclopedia's worth of knowledge about the intricacies of cars and trucks—all sorts of technical details and obscure procedures. Chris the Second nodded along, although something in his eyes suggested he was growing increasingly baffled and was uncomfortable because he didn't know what she was talking about.

"And there goes her chance at love," Kurt lamented, shaking his head sadly even as he bit down the corner of his lip to keep from smiling. He drained the last of the Coke from his glass and then used it to gesture at the eldest brother. "I blame Jacob."

Jacob snorted. "Hey, now. Learning vehicular maintenance and how to improve cars is a noble calling, in addition to being a useful skill. People make a *living* off that shit. Besides, who was it got her into fighting and whetted her taste for *that?*"

He and Kurt both looked at Russell, not bothering to venture answers, and not expecting one. It was pretty much a rhetorical question.

The tallest of the trio shrugged his huge shoulders. "It was either fight with her or put up with her wanting to play 'tea party' with me. What would you have done?"

Russell's voice was so deep it was almost a thunderous rumble. Hearing it, Cheryl, the newer waitress who'd been there when the brothers had first sauntered in, shivered despite herself.

The second woman, Tomi, had just gotten her apron on, and could not help noticing her coworker sneaking glances at the brothers, the huge Russell in particular.

Tomi sauntered up to Cheryl and put her face just above her shoulder, lips aimed at her ear.

"Why do you think I've kept this dead-end job for all these years?" she whispered. "The eye candy, and ear candy too, is worth another hundred dollars a week, minimum."

Cheryl tried not to blush. "I can understand that." She'd already encountered Jacob a few times, and it always made her day when he actually spoke to her beyond just the formalities. Now, though, she wasn't sure if she liked him or Russell better.

Tomi snickered and pretended to adjust her apron. "Well, if you do move on for greener pastures, you ought to make sure you have a list of local girls who'll want to be notified when the position becomes vacant. Some of them will even pay you money for the privilege. Helps them get a jump on the competition to fill your spot."

The younger waitress did blush now, although she had to acknowledge that Tomi had made a damn good point.

Both women strolled toward the side of the bar, headed for the break area, where Cheryl would take five minutes to have herself a drink and Tomi would finish the preparations for her shift.

Tomi added an extra tidbit to the conversation they'd had a moment ago. "You know, there's already a few other gals with money down on this, and not people you'd necessarily expect." She laughed.

Cheryl smiled. "Oh, really?"

"Yup. And Mr. Quaile, he don't mind the fights too much as long as nobody gets killed or anything like that. It brings in customers. Boys come in after Bailey, and so do her brothers," she explained. "And then all the ladies come in after Jacob and Russell and Kurt."

They disappeared into the rear corner where the small break table was set up, and Cheryl laughed openly as she took a seat. "Makes sense." She grabbed the water bottle she'd left there and took a swig as Tomi checked her makeup in a pocket mirror.

Back out in the dining-and-drinking area, Chris the Second had excused himself from the premises. Bailey finished her beer with an appreciative "ahh," and placed the bottle firmly on the bar. Mr. Quaile retrieved it at once and added it to the empties tub.

Kurt looked at her. "You know, alcohol has a drying effect," he pointed out. "So really, after all that exercise, you ought to be hydrating with some good old-fashioned water."

Bailey snorted and ruffled her younger brother's hair. "Be quiet, Kurt. It's not the same thing as whiskey. Beer's mostly water anyway, isn't it? Besides, I'm out of here."

Jacob raised an eyebrow. "Where you headed?"

She put her hands on her hips and her hazel eyes went distant. "Think I'm gonna go back to the shop," she answered him. "Clear my head and relieve some stress after all this nonsense. I swear, a girl can't even come in for a morning beer anymore without having to deal with idiots like those guys."

Quaile the bartender waved to her. "You can come in for a beer anytime you want, Bailey. Just do like the officer said and don't bust things up too much. You're good for business, and we all know you're well over twenty-one."

She waved back without looking at him and turned to leave. Something the man had just said seemed to have rankled her.

Tomi stood near the door in a position where she could

delay Bailey's exit, forcing her to acknowledge her but not *technically* blocking her.

The waitress caught the younger woman's eye. "Bailey, dear, pardon my asking, but, how old are you, again? I don't recall."

Bailey frowned, and again her eyes took on a distant cast, as though her mind were far away. The next Gathering of the Packs would be happening sooner than she'd like.

Rather than answer Tomi's question directly, she just said, "Not twenty-five. Not yet."

CHAPTER TWO

G unney's Auto Repair Shop was less than half a mile from the Bristling Elk, so Bailey just walked. It was a cool day, mostly cloudy and with scattered showers that dropped proper rain for a few minutes, then misted for half an hour, and then went dry, only to return an hour later and repeat the whole process.

That was nothing new here, and Bailey wasn't afraid of the great outdoors or the natural elements. Braving them was in her blood.

The Bristling Elk lay on Main Street, which ran through the center of town—the lowest, flattest part of the valley. From there, almost anyplace else was going to be at least slightly uphill.

Her path took her a short way down Main, then she hung a left and walked down 7th Street for a quarter mile or so, passing the gun store and the hardware store, as well as the office of a small regional credit union, the road undulating as it sloped upward into the Cascade foothills.

The mountains, thickly forested with pines of dark emerald and swathed in white mist, loomed ahead.

A kid on a bike aged ten or so rode by in the opposite direction, gravity lending him speed beyond what his legs could do. His hair and coat flapped in the damp, chilly air. He caught sight of Bailey and waved a hand at her as he flashed by.

She returned the gesture, then turned to look after him. "Be careful," she shouted. If he didn't start braking, he might burst out into the main road too fast to stop if a car was coming. She stopped to watch him. To her relief, he killed his speed near the intersection and then took a right, rather than crossing the street.

A couple of minutes later, the shop appeared, squatting comfortably on a broad and otherwise empty lot. It was separated from a nearby residential neighborhood by just enough of a state-owned, wooded slope to avoid any trouble with the zoning commission.

Most of the building was a faded ivory color, although a stripe near the top of the structure, as well as the logo, were bright red to make the place more visible to those who might need its services. Nothing about it was fancy, but it didn't need to be. Just stepping onto the lot felt like coming home.

Bailey saw that all three bays were open, and cars sat on all three of the lifts. It looked like they were only working on the two to the left, but Gunney and his boys probably meant to move on to the third within the hour.

She quickly identified the vehicles. On the left was a dark blue '96 Toyota Camry; not the most exciting car, but a reliable one, and it appeared that the owner had tried to take good care of it. Most people in these parts took vehicle maintenance seriously and attempted to hold on to their rides for as long as they reasonably could.

Next, up on the central lift, was something a little more interesting: a '95 Ford F-150 pickup truck, two-tone. The colors were divided horizontally across the body, the lower half of the truck being cherry-red, and the top half snowy-white. Something about it reminded her of an oversized peppermint.

In her opinion, it would have looked cooler with red on top and white on bottom, but that'd put the white part closer to all the dirt and mud hereabouts. She had to respect the owner's decision.

Finally, on the left was a maroon Chevy Blazer, apparently ancient. She couldn't determine the year just by looking at the damn thing. Mildly embarrassing, but it wasn't one of her favorite models, and even she couldn't keep track of everything.

Besides, she somehow suspected that it belonged to someone from out of town. Greenhearth didn't get many visitors, but occasionally someone from a neighboring town would bring their vehicle in for cheaper repairs than what they could get at home.

Or, alternately, "mountain virgins" from Seattle or Portland or California would pop their shitty tires trying to get up a winding dirt road to a scenic overlook or something and have to haul their cars in. Gunney took all comers.

In front of her, a full-timer named Gary emerged from the front office, carrying a candy bar he'd bought from the vending machine. He was apparently on his way back to the pit. "Hi, Bailey," he greeted her. "I thought this was your day off."

"Hi," she replied. "It is, but don't tell Gunney that. He doesn't need to know."

Chuckling, Gary disappeared behind the F-150.

Bailey approached the bays and saw Gunney standing next to the Camry, half-leaning against the wall and looking over a clipboard. Presumably it held the sheet that summed up the vehicle's current ills. She was pretty sure he'd heard or even sensed her coming, but he didn't look up just yet.

She spoke first. "Hey, Gunney. What's up? You need any help?" She stood, waiting in her sweater and jeans and boots, hands in her pockets.

"Maybe," he mumbled, distracted. Then he looked up and his bright green eyes focused on her.

Gunney was probably between fifty and fifty-five. Bailey had never bothered to ask him how old he was, although he was of an age with her father. In fact, someone who didn't know any better might wonder if perhaps he *was* her father.

Both the man and the girl had dark brown hair, although Gunney's, along with his beard, had turned the color of dull iron in many places and had fallen out entirely in others. There was a similar earthy toughness to their features and in the way they carried themselves. Both spoke using some of the same turns of phrase.

The one area in which they didn't resemble each other was in height, at least relative to their respective sexes. Gunney was about an inch shorter than Bailey. He claimed to have been taller in his youth.

"So," he began, his tone more jovial than his words, "what are you doing here? Trying to sabotage my business? I'm almost positive I recall giving you today off. Why don't you head down to the Elk?"

His eyes twinkled, and he removed his navy-blue baseball cap and wiped his brow with the cleaner part of a rag he'd been using to rub away oil residue. The hat slid back onto his head with the perfect ease of familiarity.

"Gunney, dammit," Bailey stated, "I just came from the Elk. How do you think I got this?" She pointed to the bruise on her cheek. "That whole business kinda left a sour taste in my mouth. There's just no escape from assholes anymore, I swear. Around this place, people are at least a little more civilized."

One of the other mechanics, who had apparently been listening to them, burst out in snorting, barking laughter at that. Bailey extended her middle finger in his general direction but kept her eyes on Gunney.

The older man smiled in a faint, wistful fashion. "I take it you didn't get into any serious trouble. Mighty nice of the sheriff's deputies to cut you some slack. Anyway, what else is on your mind?"

"Shit," she countered, "I don't even know. Everything, I guess." She kicked an empty motor oil bottle out of the walking path and toward the big metal trash can in the corner, where no one would be liable to trip over it.

"I see." Gunney nodded. "Well, the Camry here needs the truck to come in before we can get to it, and the F-150 is just minor stuff, so I ain't in a hurry at the moment."

Bailey shrugged. "I guess… I don't know. Sometimes I just get tired of the fact that everyone in this valley—hell, this whole section of the mountains—seems to know who I am and everything about me. You know? Also, what's with the candy-cane paint job on that truck? Little too much holiday spirit if you ask me."

The mechanic glanced to the side. "It's *solid* red and *solid* white. It ain't a mass of swirly stripes. Not sure why it makes you think of a candy cane. Anyway, the paint job is none of our business. Just the oil and the filter. Oh, and the oxygen sensor."

She made a sour, pouty face. "Yeah, yeah, fair enough, old man. Gotta be all respectful to the customers."

He waved one of his thick, callused hands. "Anyway, I know what you mean. About people knowing too much about you, that is. Well, more or less. I grew up down in Bend. It was a lot smaller back then, and everyone knew everyone else. Everyone talked about everyone else. By the time I was about your age, I'd just about had enough of it."

Bailey moved closer to him and leaned against the wall, just as he was doing. "Is that why you came up here?"

He gave a roll of his shoulders that wasn't quite a shrug. "Sort of. Had a few other stupid adventures first. I like it here; it's nice and quiet. Of course Bend is a goddamn metropolis compared to this town, so everyone here knows me *again* now. I can live with that, though. I'm older, and I don't make the same mistakes I used to. Makes it easier."

Bailey frowned. "You know I can't just up and leave, Gunney. It's not the same."

His face fell, but warmth and sympathy emanated from it. "True enough. Regular old humans have an easier time relocating. For what it's worth, I understand some of what you're dealing with."

While the girl brooded, the older man gave her an off-kilter smirk. "Being young mostly sucks, to be honest. It's overrated, from what I recall."

Bailey put a hand over her eyes. He was trying to make her feel better, but he didn't seem to fully grasp the situation.

"*Everyone*," she blurted in exasperation, "knows that my twenty-fifth birthday is coming up. Even Tomi at the Elk. And everyone knows what that means and won't let me forget it. Marriage. I have to get married to some dickhead. Pack rules, traditions, and all that other shit that apparently there's no escape from *ever*. Not for me, even if most of the people in our part of the world have moved on from that kind of thinking. None of that matters to Weres."

She'd surprised herself with how much she'd blurted out and how much emotion had forced its way out of her mouth. Also with the force and bitterness of her words. It was as though years' worth of built-up insecurity, resentment, and frustration had all finally crystallized and demanded to be said aloud.

Halfway embarrassed, Bailey looked at the Dale Earnhardt memorial poster on the wall, then through the window into the cozy office where Gunney received his customers. And where Gary bought his candy bars.

The mechanic shook his head and made a low sound in his throat. Nothing in his demeanor was judgmental toward her for what she'd just said.

"Different people have different customs, I guess. That's

how it's always been. I'm right there with you, though. It don't make much sense."

Bailey looked down and absentmindedly kicked at the floor, since she was fresh out of empty motor oil bottles. "Well, thanks. 'Don't make much sense' is putting it mildly, though."

"If you ask me," Gunney added, "marriage is even more overrated than youth. Well, I never been married, so I can't really say from experience, whereas I have been young, believe it or not. But getting hitched just seems like more trouble than it's worth."

Bailey shook the hair free of her shoulders, relishing the slight breeze it created. "So, it's not just me, then. Glad to hear *someone* recognizes the inherent stupidity of it."

The old mechanic shrugged. "A wedding is like taking something that should just be a personal matter and turning it into this big legal ceremony, you know? Then both parties get unrealistic expectations and start thinking about their relationship in legalistic terms, and if they ain't happy with one or two things, they treat it like a breach of contract. That's where the problems come in. I don't know. It was never for *me*, that much I can say for sure."

The girl took a moment to chew on and digest his words. "I think you hit the nail on the head, Gunney. Bunch of meddling and lawyer shit, that's all it is, really. You were smart never to get ensnared."

He laughed in a low, soft voice. "Maybe it works fine for some people, but for certain others, definitely not. Besides, who'd want a crusty old fuck like me?"

Bailey squinted at him, biting her tongue. "Watch your language around me, you filthy old man," she quipped, and she prodded his foot with the toe of one of her boots. "Last thing I need is your corrupting influence."

"Hah!" He scoffed. "Your mouth is every bit as filthy as mine half the time. Maybe more so. Although, come to think of it," he tapped his whiskery chin and pretended to look off into space with a deep, philosophical expression, "my 'corrupting influence' might possibly have had something to do with that."

She grinned in a way some people might describe as wolfish. "So you admit it! See, anytime I'm not channeling you, I'm a lady. It's my natural state."

"A lady?" he retorted, gazing at her and smirking. "Bailey, you're a bitch."

The girl burst out laughing, both of them knowing full well that he was likely the only man on Earth, at least outside of her family and pack, who could get away with that little remark.

Glancing at him out of the sides of her eyes, she shot back, "Gunney, you say the truest things. Most of the time, anyway. But you'd better mean that in the sense of me being a female Were and not the other kind."

They also both knew that the four dipshits at the Elk this morning weren't the first guys she'd beaten up for that kind of language.

As she eyed him, he scratched his chin, his lined face calm. "Hmm, well, not today, at least." The corner of his mouth threatened to shoot upward again.

Bailey put her hands on her hips. "I guess that's as good as I'm gonna get." She huffed. He was only teasing, but right now she'd rather have him warm than funny. At least he was capable of both.

"For now," the older man added, "try going an entire week without getting into a fight. It might help your reputation around here."

"Yeah, yeah," she mumbled, looking at the floor again.

"Anyway," Gunney went on, "I've got an oil and filter change coming up. If you got nothing better to do, you might as well join me. Not that I'm trying to make you 'work without pay,' of course, since I recall you were the one who offered to help."

Bailey laughed. "Yeah, we all know the score, old man. Trying to exploit the desperate citizens of this town for their cheap labor. I don't know why I fall for your schemes."

The mechanic snorted and turned his head aside as if speaking to some invisible person across from Bailey. "*Cheap labor*," he muttered, shaking his head. "Grab me the right box wrench, will you?" He set down the clipboard and strolled over to the two-tone F-150.

Bailey turned to the tool rack and readily snatched the proper implement. "You ought to get it yourself. Lazy bastard." Hefting the wrench, she followed him to the truck.

He took it from her and started examining the vehicle's undercarriage. "So, how's Tomi doing, anyway? And that new gal? What is her name?"

"Cheryl," said Bailey. "Tomi's about the same as ever. Cheryl's okay, I guess. Seems like she mostly works mornings, so she's only had to deal with the regulars who come in for breakfast. Or me and my brothers wanting a drink to start the morning off right. Wouldn't know how she handles the night rush, if she's been around for that."

"I see." Gunney nodded. He wasn't looking at her, but she knew he was legitimately paying attention.

Bailey went on, "And of course, Cheryl keeps trying to brush up against Jacob. And her and Tomi talk about them when they think I can't hear. Not my business, but well, it gets old. All four of us seem to get a little too much attention."

"Right." The mechanic started to loosen the oil pan drain bolt. "Well, you could always try distracting those gals with other gossip from around town. I heard that Maddie Foster—you remember her?—might be getting divorced from Tom soon. Not sure why, although they never struck me as being a happy couple."

Bailey, without needing to be asked, grabbed an empty pan to catch the old oil once it began to flow. "Just more evidence that marriage is a bad idea, I guess," she remarked.

Gunney chuckled and finished with the bolt. The old oil, black and thick and well below the recommended minimum level, drained into the pan as Bailey held it up.

"Let's see," the older man mused, "what else has been up?"

It occurred to Bailey that he was trying to get her mind off of her problems and distract her from the pressures of her people and their ideas about mandatory weddings and pack loyalty. She knew he was doing it, but it was a nice gesture.

"Oh," Gunney said then, "there was that little girl from the south side who went missing a couple days ago. Everyone's pretty worried since they don't have any real leads or trace of her. They've been out looking, but so far, nothing.

The sheriff sent it up the pipeline, and they put out an alert statewide. Lots of prayers being said."

Bailey frowned. "Damn. I hope they find her. She might've just gotten lost in the woods and stumbled into someone's shed for the night, and is trying to get home as we speak. But you never know."

"No," Gunney agreed, "you don't. Later, I'm gonna get a card for everyone at the shop here to sign. I know someone at church who knows her parents and they will pass it on."

"That's good of you," Bailey opined. "Missing children and potential divorces. Anything *good* going on?"

The oil finished draining, and Bailey set the pan off to the side, then snatched a filter wrench, returning to the underside of the truck.

"Yeah," Gunney answered her. "My cousin's boy Justin finally won a scholarship. He dropped out of high school, you know, so he had to earn his GED and then go through all kinds of rigmarole. Just a small one, but he's off to Salem come the fall."

"Justin?" Bailey inquired. She reached up with the wrench and fitted it on the filter. "He was in the Elk this morning. He just turned twenty-one, didn't he?"

Gunney nodded. "That he did."

"He'll have plenty more places to drink in Salem, I imagine, but nice of him to give Mr. Quaile a few dollars first."

They removed the old filter, and Gunney held down the proverbial fort as Bailey tossed it. Then she looked around for a new one. Unfortunately, some dumbass had put them behind a crate filled with old scrap parts. It was about two and a half feet cubed, and probably weighed a good hundred and ten pounds. There were scrape marks on the floor from the guys pushing it back and forth.

Bailey squatted, grabbed the crate by its sides, and lifted it chest-high as she stood up. Then she walked it over to an empty corner and easily set it down there, where it would be out of everyone's way before coming back and selecting the new filter. Gunney watched her and shook his head, a faint smile on his face.

"Hell," he commented, "I might be able to give you a couple more hours just to have you lift things for us."

"Oh," she countered, handing him the part, "have me do all the dirty work and brute force manual labor. I see."

He handed her the bolt, smirking, but for now, they were done speaking. Not because either was angry or bored, but because they'd settled into a good rhythm of steady, comfortable, purposeful work, side by side.

She put the bolt back in and tightened it with the wrench, her hands moving quickly and smoothly with the confidence of experience. Gunney's own movements made short work of the replacement filter. He hand-tightened it to satisfaction. That just left the oxygen sensor.

Bailey stood aside as the older man examined it.

"These goddamn things," he grumbled. "Always going bad around here, at least for this owner. I swear, this is the third time I've had to change his sensor in the last five years. Maybe four. What the hell has he been doing to the poor things?"

The girl shrugged. "Beats me." He likely hadn't expected an answer, but still.

A few moments later, Gunney had pulled the old one and plugged a new one in, and that was that.

"Bailey," he began, "wanna grab the keys and drive this one out back? Put it next to the black Dodge. On the far side of it, I mean. After you do that, I figure we can get something to drink."

"Sure." She strolled back and located the appropriate keys as Gunney lowered the truck to floor-level with the lift. She got the engine running, and she reversed into the big rear gravel lot, parking the vehicle just where he'd indicated.

They met by the rear door of the office. Gunney looked oddly apologetic.

"I'm fresh out of orange soda," he admitted. "So, what do you say we take a short drive to the convenience store?"

Bailey smiled. "Sounds good to me. They still got 'em in glass bottles, right? It's not the same, drinking out of plastic."

Gunney shrugged as they walked over to his truck, an F-150 not unlike the peppermint wonder they'd just worked on, though uniformly brown in his case. "As far as I know, yeah."

When they returned fifteen minutes later with a twelve-pack of orange pop, Gary was talking to someone on the shop's landline phone.

"Yeah," he said into the receiver, "you can probably come in about two and handle the oil changes for the rest of the day. Get you a few hours."

Bailey's face scrunched. "Oh, God. Is that Emily he's talking to?"

"I think so," Gunney confirmed.

They'd hired Emily two weeks ago, and it seemed like she still wasn't through the mixture of hazing and being handled with kid gloves that always seemed to apply to the new guy. Or new girl.

"Gary," Bailey called, "why not have her help you with that Blazer? She's barely worked this week."

He said goodbye and hung up before he turned to acknowledge her. "Well, she's new." He shrugged.

"I know that," the girl retorted, her tone grumpy, "but she's got bills to pay, same as the rest of us. She's gonna have to start turning tricks on the street corner to earn enough to live this way, you heathens."

Gary started to look defensive, although he also seemed to be trying not to laugh. "It's a rite of passage. You know, a tradition. No one can be trusted to be a mechanic until we're confident they can at least handle an oil change."

"Which she has," Bailey observed, raising a finger. "I'll take her on as my apprentice if I have to."

From down in the pit, another voice joined the conversation, and Bailey finally recognized it.

"See?" the other man jeered. "I told you. She's a Dark Lord of the Sith, and now she's taking on an apprentice. Always two there are, no more, no less. The evil counterpart to the Jedi."

Bailey picked up a pipe thick enough that it barely fit in her hand. "I'll shove this pipe up your ass, Kevin," she called, her voice echoing as it descended. "Then you'll have something to think about besides *Star Wars*."

"Ooooh," Kevin retorted, "not the pipe!"

Before Gunney could intervene, a white car pulled up

out front, and out stepped a familiar-looking fortyish lady. She was one of the shop's regular customers, as Bailey recalled.

Gunney went into the office to receive the woman, and Bailey trailed behind him. She wasn't *angry* at Gary and Kevin—they were her friends—but since she hadn't been in the best mood for most of the morning, she'd rather not linger on arguments.

"Hi, Monica," Gunney greeted the newcomer. "How can I help you?"

"Hi, Gunney." The woman ran a hand through her hair. "You think you could squeeze my daughter in for a checkup before tomorrow evening? She's got the Corolla. She's driving to San Francisco in a couple days, and I'm worried about her. Don't want her breaking down somewhere in California." She rolled her eyes.

The mechanic nodded. "Very likely. Just bring her in as soon as you can. I got two vehicles I have to finish today, but shouldn't take too long, and nothing much lined up after that."

Monica was about to say something, probably thank him, but then Bailey caught her eye.

"Hey," she began, "you okay, Miss Nordin? I heard about the fight. Supposedly the cops and an ambulance got involved."

Bailey clenched her jaw. Word certainly spread fast in a town with barely a thousand people, and that was including the folks who lived in the woods in the hills outside the town limits.

"Yeah," she replied in a monotone. "I'm fine."

"Well, good," Monica went on. "I worry about you,

though. If stuff like this keeps happening, don't mind my saying, but it might make it harder for you to end up mated to someone from a good pack."

Gunney visibly winced at the woman's comment.

"Oh," Bailey grated, "that's a relief. Just means I have to kick a few more asses to keep from giving mine up. I prefer it that way."

Gunney snorted with suppressed laughter and shook his head as the woman blinked in surprise and discomfort. She clearly didn't know how to respond.

Gunney stepped in front of Bailey and put a hand on Monica's shoulder. "Anyway, I promise you a slot as soon as your girl can make it in. You know you always have a place here, even if my employees can get a bit...earthy, at times." He chuckled, doing his best to blow the whole thing off as a joke.

"Okay, well," said Monica, "thanks. I'll text her and tell her to come straight here after school."

She seemed about to turn and leave, but then something occurred to her. "Oh, it's none of my business, but it seems the Elk isn't the only business the sheriff's office has had so far today. Some out-of-towner stumbled through and caused trouble, and now they're holding him down at the station. Kinda strange."

Gunney and Bailey both nodded, brows furrowed with curiosity. Strangers were not a common occurrence here, at least beyond the ones who simply passed through. It was unusual for a non-local to linger long enough to draw attention to themselves, especially if it ended with them getting arrested.

The girl rubbed the bruise on her cheek. "That's interesting."

Gunney looked sidelong at her. "Probably none of anyone's business, but if you're determined to check it out, I can't stop you."

"That's right," Bailey agreed, "you can't. Today's my day off, after all."

"Just don't cause any more trouble," the older man admonished.

Bailey put her hands on her hips. "Do I ever?"

Gunney and Monica exchanged glances. Much to her annoyance, they replied in unison, "All the time."

The mechanic added, "If this fella's in trouble, we don't want you ending up in a cell with him."

Bailey snorted. "Like I can't take care of myself."

She strode past them and out the office door, headed for the station.

CHAPTER THREE

Bailey stepped through the front door and immediately picked out the stranger.

He was seated in a chair in the front lobby—noticeably removed from easy access to the door, but not languishing in a jail cell. He wasn't even handcuffed. Clearly, he couldn't have caused that much trouble. Bailey was almost disappointed. It would have been more interesting if some sort of violence was involved.

She gave him a cursory glance, just long enough for him to notice her, and then she looked straight ahead at the desk and took a couple of steps forward.

The man was moderately tall, about six feet, lean but fit, clean-shaven and blond-haired. He was probably in his late twenties, but it was hard to say based on the brief look she'd gotten. His clothes were unremarkable: blue jeans held up by a leather belt, a red t-shirt, and a black jacket.

And there was something else about him. It wasn't merely that he was handsome. Despite his threads being no different from what anyone else around here might wear, he seemed almost classy. He had an air of sophistication, one might say. She wasn't used to encountering people like him around Greenhearth.

No one was behind the desk, but after a moment, a door opened and one of the deputies wandered out. Bailey recognized him; he hadn't been at the diner earlier, which was probably for the best.

He looked up from a sheaf of papers in his hands. "Hi there, Miss Nordin. Glad to see you just got the one bruise. How can I help you?"

She ignored his second comment and tried not to look annoyed by it. "Hi, Officer Smolinsky." She motioned to the side, around the corner of the desk, and stepped in that direction.

The deputy followed her, and she leaned close to him once they were out of obvious earshot of the newcomer.

"I'm curious," she began, "who that guy is. Someone mentioned that a stranger stopped here and managed to get himself hauled in. What did he, you know, do?"

It occurred to her that it sounded weird, and possibly even suspicious, to just ask like that, but she wasn't about to admit that she found the man strangely attractive.

Smolinsky looked skeptical, but probably not to the point of seriously questioning her motives. The brief flash of interest in his blue eyes faded.

"His name's Roland Something-or-Other," he explained. "He's not under arrest, technically. Just brought him in 'cause he was speeding and seems to have an attitude problem. Sheriff Browne pulled the guy over and he tried to get out of it, acting all cocky and shit, and gave the sheriff lip. Well, you know how he is when perps get like that. Plus I guess the sheriff checked something else—maybe past record, but I don't know yet—and decided to bring Mr. Roland in for a nice peaceful talk."

Bailey shot a quick glance over her shoulder. If the newcomer could overhear them, he'd given no indication.

"Especially," the deputy went on, "since he's a stranger around here. You know how it is."

The girl nodded. "That I do."

Behind her, heavy footsteps came out into the lobby from the building's interior. Probably the sheriff, come to ask a few more questions of their guest.

"Say," Bailey added, "you think I could sit in? Watch the guy being questioned? I'm curious, is all. Or maybe I could talk to him myself."

Smolinsky shrugged. He looked past her and squinted before he answered, "I don't see why not. Don't really care, truth be told. I have to head out in a few minutes, and you're well-known around here. As long as the sheriff doesn't object."

Bailey was about to turn around when the deputy added, "And don't cause trouble, obviously."

She grinned. "Do I ever?"

He fixed her with a level stare that almost reminded her of Gunney's. "All the time. This morning, for example. I was here when they sent Jurgensen and Etain to the diner. Let's not have a repeat of that while you're in the police station. Would make it all too easy for us to just book you and be done with it."

Bailey scowled, choosing not to respond to his words, and pivoted to head back toward the newcomer. The footsteps had indeed belonged to Sheriff Browne, who was now blocking the young man from her sight. She hung back a bit and off to the side, just close enough to see and hear what was going on without seeming to intrude.

The sheriff cleared his throat. "Let me get this straight. You're from Seattle, and earlier you said you sometimes have business in Portland. What are you doing out *here?* We're a small town in the mountains, well off the beaten path, and a good hour *southeast* of Portland. If you were headed back home, you sure went the wrong way."

The man shrugged. His face was almost totally devoid of expression. "I can afford to lose an hour or two. I'm not in any hurry to get back home."

Browne hooked his thumbs in his belt. He was a large, imposing man, at least as tall as Bailey's brothers Jacob and Kurt (although not as tall as Russell), and almost twice as wide as any of them. His black mustache bristled.

"Son," he observed, his tone more curious than accusatory, "you don't seem like the type who'd find much to interest you in our little hamlet. It's strange, don't you think? If you were looking for fun, you'd have been better off either staying in Portland, or going up to Mount Hood or something. So, what brings you to Greenhearth?"

His face a picture of perfect innocence, Roland responded, "Oh, I just needed to clear my head after a long night. Went out for a relaxing drive in the countryside on a public road that anyone is allowed to drive on."

Bailey bit her tongue to keep from snickering. The stranger had an attitude, but not a loud or blatant one.

The sheriff sighed. "I was hoping you'd be more cooperative. I can't book you for just going six over the speed limit, but that doesn't mean you're free to go just yet. I got a nose for trouble, young man, and I suspect you're exactly that, or that you've somehow brought it with you. Frankly, we already have our share of trouble, small as we are. Don't need more."

Leaning back, he caught Bailey in the corner of his eye, and a sly smile grew beneath his mustache. Then he turned and plodded back into the office.

"Just stay put, now," he called back, his voice trailing off.

Bailey frowned, trying not to visibly huff at the implication that she was the trouble he'd alluded to. For the most part, she was a pillar of this community. The only time there were problems was when assholes got in her way, harangued her, or disrespected her. That was all.

Rather than dwell on the subject, she plopped into a chair next to Roland.

"Hi," she opened.

"Hello there," he replied, his voice mid-range and smooth. "Somehow I don't think you're an officer of the law."

"Not quite." She crossed her arms over her chest. "Just a concerned citizen."

He nodded. "In that case, could you tell me why I have to sit here when I'm not even being charged with anything, and I'm not even restrained? It doesn't make sense. I could just walk out the door if I wanted."

"Eh," Bailey remarked, "I wouldn't attempt that. They'd catch you again quick, and then they *would* be able to book you for resisting arrest or some crap."

He leaned back and put his hands behind his head. "Fair enough. I'll just do nothing, then, until they let me go." He closed his eyes as if preparing for a nap.

The girl wasn't going to let him off that easily. "I'm Bailey," she introduced herself. "I hear you're Roland."

He opened his eyes and turned them toward her without moving his head. "Nice to meet you, Bailey. And you heard correctly."

Awkward silence set in as the man looked at the ceiling.

Not discouraged, Bailey pressed on. "Come on, now. I'm curious what you're doing here, too, and why the sheriff brought you in when he could have just wrote you a speeding ticket and called it good."

Roland sat back up straight. "Oh, so you *are* law enforcement. Undercover good cop, counterbalancing the sheriff in the bad cop role."

Bailey scoffed. "No, I'm not."

"Well, I'm sticking to my story," Roland proclaimed. "I felt like taking a drive through the country, so I did. I just happened to drive slightly too fast at the wrong time."

Bailey half-grimaced. "Fair enough. What's the business you have in Portland, though? You a businessman, or do you just have an old roommate there you play *Dungeons &* *Dragons* with once a month or something like that?"

He shrugged. "No comment."

Now she was getting frustrated. It must have been obvious since Smolinsky strolled by on his way out and added his two cents.

"I'd tell her what she wanted to know there, young man." He paused to zip up his jacket.

Roland raised his eyebrows. "Oh? Why should I?"

The deputy smirked. "As a wise man once said, always let the Wookie win." He nodded at Bailey, then trudged out the front door.

The girl's teeth clenched; he'd stopped just short of telling Roland what she was, not that he was likely to figure it out. She calmed down by imagining Smolinsky and Kevin back at the shop having a long, nerdy, annoying conversation about *Star Wars* stuff for half a day, keeping both men distracted and out of everyone else's hair.

Roland turned his face toward Bailey now, the seed of legitimate curiosity sown. "Wookie? That's interesting. You don't *look* all that furry."

"You're observant," Bailey quipped. "He's right, though. I can and will pull your arm out of its socket. Best start talking, boy." She allowed herself to smile a little at this to soften the implied threat.

He drew his arms closer to his torso as if trying to protect them. "I see. Okay, then. I help run a family business of sorts back in Seattle. We know some people in Portland who run a complementary business, and I sometimes head south to negotiate deals with them. I have some extra time, so I thought I'd see the mountains in Oregon. Is that good enough?"

"It's a start." Bailey shrugged. "We need better gossip material than that around here, though. Or at least I do, although I don't gossip much. I think in this case I'd rather just keep it all to myself."

She allowed her gaze to linger on him until he replied, and she knew that, at this moment, something in her eyes was changing. He might be perceptive enough to notice it.

His own eyes were dark blue, almost violet. Two guys came in just then and stood by the desk, probably waiting to pay a parking ticket or something. Neither Roland nor

Bailey looked away from each other, and he only blinked once.

"I can see I'm not going to get out of this after all, am I?"

Bailey smirked. "Nope."

"So be it." Roland cracked his neck. Then, with the air of a man who figured no one would believe him anyway, he told the true story of why he was here.

"I'm what you might call a wizard," he said flatly. "The power is inborn, although knowledge and study and practice can develop it further. I made a few mistakes and became too well-known around Seattle. I'm all the way out here because I'm trying to get the hell away from a gaggle of awful cutthroat witches."

Bailey stared, and realized after a second that her jaw was hanging open. The two bros who'd just come in were also glancing at Roland with quizzical, amused expressions.

"You see," the blond stranger went on, "they over-focus on the hereditary aspect. Based on my reputation and a brief in-person assessment, they essentially just want me for my body, and for purely selfish reasons on their part—to birth a new generation of witches or wizards, who will be further empowered by my, you know, contribution. Since the seed is strong, if you don't mind my saying so, it makes whatever talents their children get much stronger they would otherwise have been, based on my family's history. Strength and power are everything in the magical community."

The two guys exchanged glances and seemed on the verge of butting into the conversation, but then the sheriff approached from the other side of the desk and stole their attention.

Bailey, meanwhile, remembered to close her mouth.

"Jesus H. Christ," she said softly. "That was not what I expected to hear. I don't know what I *did* expect, but it wasn't that."

Roland said nothing, his face impassive.

Bailey was on the verge of smacking him and telling him to shut up, chewing him out for making shit like that up and expecting country bumpkins would believe it, but...

He was telling the truth. There *were* things like that in the world—Bailey of all people would know—and Roland's flippancy was because he didn't care if people thought he was crazy.

"You're serious," she stated.

He spread his hands. "It's up to you if you want to believe me, but yes, I am."

All at once, a dozen thoughts fought for space and attention within Bailey's skull. She blinked and rubbed her temples, trying to impose order on them. She struggled to keep too much emotion from bursting out and making things messier still.

A few of the thoughts fell neatly into place.

Here was a man fleeing from people who wanted to force him to mate.

He was an out-of-towner, an unknown quantity. People from around here, including Weres, would not be able to pass judgment on every single thing he'd ever said or done since they'd known nothing about him until he blundered into town this morning.

If Bailey were to suddenly appear to be *dating* such a

man, people would be confused, but they'd also be satisfied. It would look like she was finally taking her responsibilities seriously.

With Roland's help, they might leave her alone at long last. She had some inkling of what it was like to be in his situation, as well. She wanted to help him on that basis alone.

Bailey drew in her breath. "Roland, believe it or not, I understand your situation better than you might guess. And, well, I suspect we can help each other."

For the first time, the man showed something resembling emotion. He snorted and swung his head down and away from her, a mixture of skepticism and gloomy pessimism on his handsome face.

"What's wrong?" she asked.

At the desk, the bros handed wads of cash to the sheriff, dutifully paying whatever fine they'd incurred for some recent bullshit infraction. Browne shot Bailey another surreptitious glance while he handled the money. He could overhear them, of course, but she didn't care.

Roland rubbed his eyes. "I appreciate the offer, but you don't know all the ins and outs. There's a lot more to it than the average person could ever understand. I don't mean to say you're not smart enough or anything like that. It's just, we're talking about a culture that most people know nothing about."

Bailey's stomach clenched as determination filled her from scalp to soles. She wasn't about to let this guy just give up right in front of her.

"Some people might know more than you think," she shot back. "And I already have a perfect cover story that might get them off your back. Not to mention, you'd be doing me a favor. Now, being detained here for the terrible crime of speeding, you've already lost some of the time you were probably going to spend trying to get farther southeast. Maybe go all the way to the High Desert or into Nevada or Idaho, is that right?"

Frowning, Roland affirmed that it was.

"Well," Bailey continued, "change of plans. Once our good sheriff lets you go, we'll talk it over. What do you say to a tentative alliance?"

He threw up his hands. "It sounds like you're not giving me much choice in the matter anyway, so sure, why not? I'll tentatively agree to hear your idea."

The pair of guys turned away from the desk and walked toward the door, slowing as they passed Bailey and Roland.

"You better, man," one of them shouted to Roland. "Sounds like you're in some deep shit. God, must be horrible, being chased by a bunch of hot women who only want you for your body."

The other one sniggered. "Right, bro. No man alive would want to be in your shoes right now. Best of luck escaping that terrible fate and all."

Bailey glared at them.

Roland just smiled. "Your sympathy is appreciated, gentlemen."

The two guys pushed open the door and disappeared into the mist.

Sheriff Browne had remained at the desk, and his eyes were on the pair in the lobby. "Bailey, like everyone else has already told you," he began, "don't cause trouble, don't go looking for trouble, and don't bring any trouble onto us that we don't need to deal with."

He paused for effect, and after a second or two of silence, shifted his eyes to the stranger. "And you, sir, are free to go, on the condition that everything I just said to the young lady applies to you as well. If you stick around in Greenhearth, we'll be watching."

Roland nodded. "Understood, Sheriff. Thanks." He stood and stretched his arms and legs.

Bailey stood up beside him. She wanted to grab his arm protectively but she stopped herself. "Come on, then. I'll tell you what I have in mind while we go to meet my brothers."

Bailey led the way into the Elk, Roland trailing behind her. She didn't wait to see if he'd have gone out of his way to hold the door for her. She was perfectly used to opening doors herself, and she had other things on her mind at the moment.

The first thing she noticed upon stepping into the dark but cozy space was that the other Nordins were not at the bar.

"Damn," she mumbled under her breath. She took about three steps in, then stopped.

Roland came up alongside her. "Well, it's noonish on a weekday. Not prime time for a drinking establishment."

"Hold on," she chided him, "they might still be around somewhere. First though, I need to get my mouth wet."

One of Roland's eyebrows shot up as he looked at her.

"Don't," she added, holding up a finger, "take that the wrong way, you filthy pervert. Just means I want something to drink."

He slipped out of his jacket and carried it over his left arm. "I'll take your word for it."

She strode up to the bar and sat down at one of the stools, waiting for Mr. Quaile or whoever else might be working by now. Using her left foot, she pushed the stool beside her out for Roland to use.

He obliged, draping his lanky frame over it and relaxing his elbows on the bar.

The bartender appeared from somewhere in back. "Back again so soon?" he inquired, his eyes jumping from her to the stranger.

"Yeah," she acknowledged. "It's been a thirsty day. Another beer, please."

He nodded. "And you, sir?"

"Oh," said Roland, "just a glass of water. And I can pay you for it; that's no problem."

"Coming right up." Quaile turned to fetch their drinks.

Bailey looked at the man who was for all intents and purposes her date. "Don't you drink? Please tell me you're not a teetotaler or straight-edge or whatever they call it."

He let out a soft, dry chuckle. "No, I drink. I'm just not in the mood for it right now."

She decided that his answer was satisfying for now. "Okay, suit yourself."

Quaile returned with a perspiring gold bottle in one hand and a clear, ice-filled glass in the other. "There you go. I'll ring up your tabs when you're done."

As they settled into their drinks, Bailey noticed that

Tomi and Cheryl had materialized at the far corner of the bar opposite the dance floor, and near the bend where the bar became the diner and were examining the newcomer.

This did not shock her. The two of them (or Tomi alone, before Cheryl had started) performed a detailed scientific survey of pretty much every man who came in, especially if he was obviously from a faraway land.

Still, she found that her off-hand was slowly clenching into a fist. Although she tried not to let it bother her, she felt like they ought to give it a rest, at least once.

To derail them, she decided to force them to do their jobs.

"Hey," she called, "Tomi and Cheryl. Lunch crowd isn't in yet, are they? I'm getting hungry. Might switch over to the diner side and order something."

"It's starting," Tomi reported. "One lady came in a few minutes after you left earlier. Then two decent-sized parties; they're finishing up though. Otherwise, right now it's just your brothers."

"Ah," she commented, "so that's where they got off to. Men, always thinking with their stomachs."

She slid down from the stool. She'd only finished half her beer, but it would be a simple matter to take it over to a table and have it added to her bill there. "Let's get something to eat," she suggested.

Roland climbed down from his own perch. "If you say so. I didn't have breakfast, so that's not a bad idea."

As they walked toward the bend, the waitresses remained where they were, their eyes on the tall blond gentleman.

"So," Cheryl said, "aren't you going to introduce us to your friend?"

Bailey's jaw muscles tightened. "He can introduce himself if he feels like it."

Apparently taking this as a prompt, Roland waved to the two women. "Hi, I'm Roland. Nice to meet you. Was just passing through, but Bailey insisted I meet her family."

He shrugged his way past them. It hadn't sounded like he was trying to be flirtatious, but you could never be sure with men.

She put a hand on his wrist and pulled him along, bodily moving him away from the staring duo.

He was, after all, her chance to relieve all the marriage pressure. Didn't want anything screwing that up. She told herself that three or four times in her head as they traversed the floor into the diner. She had to protect her investment in him; that was all.

To her slight relief, a third waitress was on duty, poised to handle any new customers.

"Hey, Judy." Bailey waved to her. "Thought we'd have some lunch. Are my brothers around? I heard they moseyed over here."

Judy was an older lady, married, and known to be straitlaced. "They sure are. Right over there, if you wanted the table next to them." She pointed.

Beyond a couple of clusters of four or five people each, mostly employees of the same companies taking their lunch breaks together, was a corner filled with high-backed booths. Judy had indicated the one just before the far wall. Bailey could barely make out Russell's head hovering above the seatback.

She led Roland toward them, and Judy trudged a few feet behind. When they were almost on top of the booth, Bailey stopped before an adjacent table. Without bothering to ask for either help or permission, she grabbed the table, which was meant to seat four people, and lifted it with one hand, and pushed it up against the table in the booth.

Her brothers turned to look at her, subdued amusement on all their faces.

"Hi, guys," she greeted them. "Mind if we join you?"

"We?" Kurt mused. He and the other two studied Roland.

Bailey gestured to her date. "This is Roland. I rescued him from whatever horrible fate the sheriff had planned for him after he caught the dumb bastard driving six over the speed limit. Let's just say he strikes me as the friendly type."

Russell studied the blond man with his usual smoldering neutral gaze, while Jacob and Kurt raised their eyebrows and smiled. Bailey and Roland took their seats, and Judy appeared to hand them menus.

"I see you already have drinks," the waitress observed. "If you want anything else right away, let me know. Otherwise, I'll be back to check on you in a couple minutes."

Roland nodded to her. "Thank you, ma'am."

"Wow!" Jacob marveled as the server hustled off. "He called Judy 'ma'am.' Where are you from, Roland?"

"Seattle," he replied.

Bailey knew they'd waste time asking him all the same questions she'd already been through at the station, so she motioned for her brothers to zip it. "We're gonna cut straight to the chase," she informed them. "Roland has a situation, and I think we can help him, just as he can help us. Well, me, at least. Roland, tell them what you told me. No need to hold back."

Roland seemed perturbed, as if he'd expected more formalities or privacy. It might have just been that he was concerned about how her brothers would react. The mere sight of the hulking trio gave a lot of men pause when it came to speaking too freely.

"Go on," Bailey urged. "They can offer us advice. Well, if they can gather enough brain cells between them to think straight." She kicked Jacob's boot under the table, and he gently kicked back. The other two rolled their eyes.

The Seattleite sighed and told his story, beginning with a quick summary of how Browne had pulled him over and detained him until Bailey had shown up.

Just before he got to the interesting part, Judy returned. "You ready to order?"

Bailey looked up. "Yeah, I'll have the steak sandwich, rare, with fries. Sauce and ketchup on the side. The usual."

While she ordered, Roland had a moment to flip open the menu. When Judy turned to him, he simply said, "I'll have the same, but cooked medium, if that's all right. Oh, and a cup of coffee. Cream on the side, no sugar, please."

Judy jotted down their orders and took the menus. "I'll get that right in for you." She turned and left.

Jacob made a sputtering sound. "*Medium.*" He scoffed. "If you'd ordered it well-done, we might've had to throw you out."

Bailey was about to tell him to shut up, but Roland just shrugged the comment off and took a sip of his ice water before resuming his story.

He told them everything. All that he'd told Bailey, and a little more, like that the witches were actively trailing him and were probably using magic to narrow down his whereabouts, although, of course, he had a few tricks of his own for obscuring his location.

When it was over, Jacob, who'd been shaking his head, slapped himself in the face.

"Fuck me." He grunted. "And I might even mean that literally, because you, sir, are a bitch. I mean, *really?* Your so-called 'problem' is that a bunch of babes want to lay you? Woooooow. I'm not sure whether I want to hit you with my car or trade places with you. Maybe both?"

Judy returned with a cup of coffee just as Jacob made this comment. She furrowed her brow but didn't interfere with the discussion. Roland thanked her and stirred creamer into his cup.

"I," Roland retorted, "don't see it that way."

Bailey shot her sibling a death glare. "Maybe you could show a little goddamn understanding, considering he's basically in the same boat as I am?"

Jacob blinked, taken aback. Kurt, too, seemed to be turning new thoughts over in his head. Russell just nodded. They'd all gotten the point, and they all cared about their sister.

Although Kurt couldn't quite help himself sometimes.

"Maybe," he quipped, "we could chop off his junk and feed it to a goat, like the Imp on *Game of Thrones* was always threatening to do."

Everyone stared at him, variously displaying bewilderment, horror, or bemusement.

"What?" he protested. "It would work. He'd live as long

as we cauterized the wound right away." He said this in an even tone as if it were obvious. "The witches would be physically incapable of banging him, so he could just go on his merry way. Everyone wins."

After a second or so of awkward silence, his face started to crack into a smirk that looked like the beginning of a bout of hysteria. "Even the goat would get a snack." Then he cracked up.

Roland shuddered. "I see." He looked at Bailey. "Is this what you call help?"

Bailey couldn't respond immediately. Her brothers refused to take things seriously, and she didn't want to resort to swearing loudly in their faces to make them behave.

Before she could attempt a more nuanced response, though, the side doors—the ones leading directly from the parking lot to the dining area—burst open. Bailey swung her head around, somehow sensing that she ought to be paying attention to the new arrivals.

There were four of them, all men she recognized, although, at other times, she'd seen women hanging around with them. All were large, with shaggy hair and unruly beards, and they wore long duster-style coats.

Her stomach sank.

"Ugh," Kurt muttered. "The South Cliff Pack."

"Yup," Jacob sighed. "Here comes trouble."

CHAPTER FOUR

Roland obviously had no way of knowing who the four guys were, but he picked up on the sudden tension and dismay easily enough. "Friend of yours?" he asked.

Bailey unwrapped her utensils and twirled the knife around her fingers. "Not exactly. Just hope our food gets here soon, so we don't have to stick around too long."

The Seattleite nodded and sipped his coffee.

Fortunately, their sandwiches arrived a moment later. No sooner had Judy set them on the table than the South Cliffs descended on a booth just across the room from the Nordins.

The tallest of them, Dan Oberlin, shouted at the waitress, "Hey! Some service over here."

Judy, startled, turned and hustled over to them. "Hello, guys. One second, and I will get you some menus."

"Yeah," another of them growled.

Bailey tried to ignore them, but she knew they'd seen

her group. The other diners, too, had already settled into uncomfortable resignation to their fate.

The South Cliff Pack was composed of Weres from three local families, all of whom were longtime fixtures in the community. That gave them a default respectability that led to them being tolerated, but even in such a small and homey place as Greenhearth, they weren't what anyone would call popular.

Bailey dug into her sandwich; she hadn't realized how hungry she'd been, and biting into some good bloody meat made her feel a hell of a lot better. To her annoyance, she saw Roland pick up a knife and fork, but relaxed once he'd cut the sandwich in half and picked up the first half to eat it the proper way.

The Nordin brothers had already finished their meals, but they stuck around, partially to continue the discussion of Bailey's plan when they could, and partially because of the South Cliffs.

They were already getting rowdy, yelling rather than talking, and a couple of them kept standing up and brushing other people who tried to walk past them, obviously not by accident. The Nordins watched the shenanigans out of the corners of their eyes.

"No one," Jacob lamented in a low whisper, "ever ousts them for this shit. They bully people and act like asses and just get away with it."

The others nodded, aside from Roland, although he paid attention to their reactions.

As Bailey and the out-of-towner neared the end of their meals, a round of grumbling speech passed around the South Cliff table, and all four of them stood up at once.

Bailey didn't turn her head, but she did focus her ears on them, paying close attention to every sound. She didn't know what they were up to, but the vibes she was getting weren't good.

Of course, the pack stomped over and came to a halt right next to the table where Bailey and Roland sat.

When the girl looked up at them, she saw that Roland was already doing so, his face open but neutral, dabbing a corner of his mouth with a napkin. Dan Oberlin, meanwhile, was staring down at them with a toothy shark's grin and glittering, flinty gray eyes.

All of a sudden, the Nordin brothers had slid out of their seats and sprang to their feet. They weren't adopting hostile postures, just interposing themselves. Dan was a little taller than Jacob or Kurt but thinner, and none of the South Cliffs were the size of Russell.

Bailey glanced up at Oberlin, and she saw the predatory grin slip off his face and dismay replace it. She looked back down at her plate, where she dabbed a steak fry into some ketchup.

"What do you want, Dan?" she asked.

By now, Dan's cronies had advanced. If the shit hit the fan, they could spring into action quickly enough, but not in time to stop their leader from being dogpiled by the Nordins.

Dan looked back down at her.

"We heard about your situation," he replied in his rugged baritone voice. "How time's running out, and you're gonna have to make a decision soon. Too bad you've turned off or scared away damn near all your suitors by ignoring your duties, taking cheap shots, shooting your mouth off, and being a bitch in general."

The three brothers winced in unison as if preparing for a thunderbolt to descend from on high.

Bailey looked back up, catching Dan's small, mean, glinting eyes with the blazing depths of her own hazel orbs. A thunderbolt was exactly what she felt building within her, and it wanted more than anything to break free and find its mark in the middle of Oberlin's face.

But she did nothing. She took a long draw of air in through her nostrils and clenched her abdominal muscles, then flexed her feet within her boots to localize the tension where no one would see it. The façade she presented was intense but controlled.

It was because of Roland. She hadn't yet outed herself to him as a Were; combat between her and another of her kind would clue him in that they weren't normal humans.

Furthermore, today was a bad day to have the cops show up again. Not only had they already been here once, but Roland had just left their tender hospitality behind, and the sheriff's warning was still fresh in both their minds. If he was present at an ugly brawl, they'd arrest him for real.

"So, what?" Bailey sneered. "You've come to offer yourself as my goddamn Prince Charming? You didn't even bring me flowers."

Dan scowled even harder. "You're running out of options, Nova," he remarked, daring to use her nickname. "There ain't a Were in this entire stretch of the mountains who's a better prospect. Real strength, and a bloodline that's proven to produce children who always change."

Now she was *really* pissed. He had outed her, damn him.

"None of you knuckle-dragging throwbacks have enough balls between the four of you to marry me," she snapped. "You'd all add up to about half of a husband." She capped it off with a mirthless animal grin, all her teeth bared.

Dan Oberlin just stared, but his minions visibly bristled. One of them, a squat and jowly guy a few years younger than Dan, stepped forward and extended a hand toward her.

Suddenly Russell was there, his huge form blocking the man.

"Try it," he rumbled, "and you'll end up in more pieces and twisted scraps than some of those miserable wrecks Gunney tows in." He paused; the entire diner had gone dead silent. "Even Bailey won't be able to put the whole stinking mess back together."

In the quiet and stillness that followed, Bailey did a quick visual scan of the premises. The other diners were assertively trying to look at nothing while turning themselves invisible. Judy had returned to check on them, but she'd stopped in her tracks halfway across the floor, waiting. No one spoke or moved.

Dan had regained enough self-control to have fallen back a step, weighed the odds, and considered how bad he and his henchmen looked, not to mention the consequences of a serious shitstorm going down in the middle of the town's most popular bar-and-eatery. Plus, the two gangs were evenly matched in numbers. Or outnumbered, if Roland counted.

The South Cliff leader snorted and waved a hairy hand. "The hell with this place. We got better things to do," he growled. He turned around and took a few steps toward the exit, the other three keeping pace with him but backing up so their eyes stayed on the Nordins.

Once he was safely out of arm's reach, Dan looked back and tried to have the last word. "Fact that she ain't even interested in men isn't a problem that concerns us," he opined. "She'd probably be a shitty lay anyhow."

Bailey couldn't let that one go. "I probably wouldn't even feel it, dipshit. Some of the girls around town say you're the size of a spark plug."

Dan turned back around slowly. "Girls say a lot of stupid things," he grumbled, and he led his cronies out the door. Everyone watched them leave.

Bailey cupped a hand by her mouth. "See ya, Sparky," she called just before the door swung shut.

Judy turned her eyes heavenward and let out a deep breath, then realized that they'd skipped out before they'd even received their orders, let alone paid for them.

The Nordins, meanwhile, settled back into their seats. Russell remained his usual quietly smoldering self, but Jacob and Kurt were now audibly groaning and rubbing their foreheads.

"Of all the goddamned shit-assed fuckery." Jacob sighed. "Life's about to get fun, boys."

Kurt joined the chorus. "Yeah. I mean, did you *have* to say the spark-plug thing? They're gonna bring down all kinds of crap on our heads over this."

Bailey scowled. "Someone's gotta stand up to those

bastards," she stated. "Besides, they were looking for trouble."

Roland, observing them as he finished the last of his fries, was curious. "Don't take this the wrong way," he inquired, "but are you afraid of them?"

The Nordins looked at him in unison, not angry, but happy to answer his question. Jacob spoke first.

"Not physically," he explained. "Hell, we'd *love* to get our hands on those numbnuts and book them a free trip to the hospital to rethink their lives for a while. It's the pack politics that are going to make our lives hell. The drama, you might say."

Kurt looked at Roland. "Yup. The Oberlins—they're the family of the charming ringleader there—they're old, respectable, and well-established, with money to burn. A lot more money than we have. They can cause some *real* trouble—worse than anything Dan Oberlin can do with his fists—if they're pushed too far. Can't solve *those* kinds of problems by just kicking everyone's asses."

The Seattleite nodded, taking all the information in, and thinking that Kurt, despite being nineteen at most, was smart for his age. He also took note of the word "pack." He had already heard Dan Oberlin say, "Weres."

For now, all he said was, "Money isn't everything."

The quintet left the diner together after they'd settled their bill and tipped Judy a bit extra for the stress caused by Dan and his little fan club. Of course, they also suggested that the diner recover the cash it had lost when the South Cliffs had walked out by sending a bill straight to the Oberlin household.

Now they walked down Greenhearth's streets. The misty rain had let up and the clouds had largely dispersed, revealing the sun for the first time that day.

Roland seemed to think it odd that he'd collected an entire entourage, and was also a mite uncomfortable with leaving his car behind. Bailey felt he could live with it for now. There was strength in numbers. If the police drove by, they'd be less likely to hassle him if he was surrounded by Nordins.

And the South Cliffs wouldn't dare attempt an ambush on all five of them at once. Not unless they'd brought the entire rest of the pack with them, and that would pretty much be all-out war. No one wanted that to happen in the middle of town.

With the privacy offered by the open air and mostly empty streets, they resumed their conversation with a little encouragement from Bailey and her brothers.

"So, Roland," she quipped, "I got the impression you had more to say before we were rudely interrupted back there. Care to finish your story?"

He ambled beside her, keeping pace with the Nordin siblings, which not many humans could do. "I can talk more or less endlessly about a bunch of different topics," he admitted, "but I'd finished my story, and we were starting to discuss…strategies? I think we'd just eliminated the one involving the goat."

Kurt snickered.

"Right," Bailey acknowledged. "Well, the gist of what I had in mind is that we can cover each other's backs. Fill in the holes in the other's story, if that makes sense. But if you can tell us anything more about your situation, then let's hear it. It'll help us make up our minds."

"Yeah," Jacob assented. "Talk about wizard stuff, or even just about Seattle. Either way, I'm sure it'll be really, *really* weird."

Roland smiled, taking the veiled insult in good humor and apparently enjoying being the center of attention.

"You asked for it," he shrugged. "For starters, Seattle is approximately one-hundred and seventy miles north of Portland, and is the largest city in the state of Washington, as well as the northernmost large city in the United States, unless you count Anchorage. It was founded in—"

Russell interrupted. "We know *that*, smartass." He grunted. "Tell us the *good* stuff."

"Wizard stuff," Jacob clarified. "Wizard stuff as pertains to Seattle."

Roland pretended to be exasperated by their requests. "Fine." He sighed.

A Sheriff's Department cruiser drove by and Bailey tensed, but it didn't slow down or stop and had soon vanished down a side street.

Roland began the next phase of his tale. He spread his hands almost theatrically as he spoke. Somehow this didn't come across as arrogant or ridiculous; it just seemed natural for him, possibly something his family did.

"I come from a wizarding line that predates the foundation of the city," he explained. "We've always kept highly detailed family records because our family is unusual. For some reason no one has quite figured out, we often produce heirs who display more magical potential than normal, frequently on the male side. That's the truly unusual part. The common wisdom has always held that witches are more inherently magical and usually reach greater heights of power."

Bailey listened with growing fascination. Given the nature of her upbringing, she knew that there were more things in the world than many regular humans chose to acknowledge, but she'd also never really been away from home. Wizards and witches in Seattle might as well have been aliens in Mongolia.

Furthermore, what he'd said about abnormally high potential cast more light on the motives of his pursuers.

"Thus," Roland continued, "those of us who are born as these 'prodigies' are considered to be especially prized marriage prospects. Whichever family gets to mingle their blood with ours also gets an uptick in power, and therefore in status."

As Bailey contemplated this, he frowned and added, "Of course, marriage isn't strictly necessary. Some people would be happy just to use me as a…stud."

Jacob broke out laughing at that. However, remembering how Bailey had reacted to his earlier wisecracks, he kept any further ones to himself.

Roland went on, "In conclusion, I'm mobile, I have enough money to last me a while, and I figured the last place a trio of ruthless, obnoxious, Machiavellian witches would think to look for me was in some Podunk little town this far from even Portland."

There was an awkward jerk in his otherwise smooth stride just then, as though he'd caught himself in some way or suddenly thought of something. He glanced at his new friends.

"Uh," he added, "sorry about the 'Podunk' thing. Didn't mean to sound condescending."

Kurt waved a hand. "Meh, don't worry about it. We *are* a smaller, out-of-the-way sort of town. Not exactly Portland, but not just two cabins in the woods, either. If you want to go someplace like *that*, we can point you in the right direction." He chuckled.

"Hmm," Roland retorted, "I'll keep that in mind. Two cabins in the woods might be overdoing it, though."

By now, the brothers were warming up to Roland, at least somewhat. Bailey was thankful for that. Making her scheme work would be a hell of a lot harder if they'd decided to hate the poor man.

Then Roland said something that shocked them all.

"Truth be told," he began, "there's another reason I chose Greenhearth. Moving in magical circles, one naturally hears about supernatural things of all sorts, and at some point, I heard this town was a haven for werewolves."

No one missed a step, but something passed between them like a spark of static electricity, and Bailey was suddenly afraid. She couldn't put a finger on why, just a general feeling of dread and anxiety.

Jacob cleared his throat. "Sounds like you hear some interesting shit. Werewolves?"

"I do," Roland confirmed. "Of course, I can't tell who is or isn't one, and the only way to find out would be to expend a great deal of magical energy on an appropriate spell, which I don't feel like doing right now. Or if I were to see one of them transform, I guess. Anyway, the important thing is that no one is going to look for a wizard in a town full of wolves."

By now, they were nearing the northern edge of the town proper. Buildings were sparser, and the trees more dense. It was quieter, with far less vehicular traffic and no pedestrians besides them. The residential area stretched on a ways before they were out into the true boonies, but there was more privacy here.

Jacob halted. "Okay, everyone stop."

They all heeded his suggestion, turning to him to hear what he had to say next.

"Roland." Jacob snapped his fingers. "No offense, but could you stand over there for a minute while we have a quick powwow? Family conference, you might say. Keep in sight, though."

Russell looked from his siblings to the wizard and back and nodded his approval.

Roland just shrugged. "Not a problem." He trudged uphill to the place Jacob had indicated, a flat grassy area where the road curved beneath a streetlamp.

The Nordins moved a few yards farther from him and huddled.

"Jacob," Bailey began, her voice a sharp whisper, "what's the problem? Why are you doing this?"

He stared at her. "Did you just *hear* that? He claims to know all about us, basically. We still don't know anything about him aside from what he told us, which for all we know might be one hundred percent pure bullshit. Hell, the Oberlins might have hired him to fuck with us, and that whole incident at the diner might have been staged to flush us out or something."

Bailey's fear from a moment ago shifted; now, she was almost furious. "Oh, come on. You know that's not true. They wouldn't have gone to *that* much trouble even before we pissed them off. I mean, yeah, they've never liked us, but their plots don't go that deep."

Russell surprised them by speaking next. "Probably not," he whispered, his voice little more than a deep vibration, "but Jacob's right about one thing. We don't know who he really is."

Kurt rubbed his chin. "Yeah. Sorry, Bailey, but we're not gonna let you run off with him alone at this point. At least until we can, you know, interrogate him or whatever a little more thoroughly."

Bailey shot a quick glance at Roland. He stood nonchalantly on the low ridge, hands in his pockets, admiring the foggy mountains that encircled the valley.

Looking back to her brothers, she grated, "Fine, escort me for my own safety for the time being, and we'll grill him a little harder. Maybe even, I don't know, check his damn driver's license. But I can usually tell when someone's lying, and I don't think he is. If he's telling the truth, I can't pass up this opportunity."

Jacob looked her in the eyes. "You like this guy already? Eh, don't answer that, sorry. But fair enough. We'll keep him around, but we're also gonna be keeping an eye on him."

"Right," she agreed hurriedly. "Wanna take him home?"

The brothers nodded.

"Okay." She stood up straight, formally ending the huddle. "Let's do that, then." Turning around, she motioned for Roland to come back down and rejoin them.

"How was your huddle?" he asked mildly.

Kurt beat her to a response. "Fantastic. Next play's a guaranteed touchdown."

Jacob poked Kurt in the ear, causing him to stumble. "Cute. But yeah, Roland, we've decided to head back to the old Nordin family castle."

Bailey added, "You're coming with us. Obviously."

CHAPTER FIVE

The family dwelling wasn't actually a castle. It probably didn't even qualify as an estate except in the strictly legal sense of being a property that had been passed down through several generations.

It lay on the northwest edge of Greenhearth's farthest mini-suburb, with a couple of other houses nearby but none behind it, only the hills. The lot was a respectable one acre, and the edifice a two-story quasi-Victorian, not quite a farmhouse but not quite a regular house, either.

Bailey was suddenly self-conscious about how old and rundown the place looked. She and her brothers kept up with repairs and resurfacing to the best of their ability, but nothing could hide its age. The place had been built almost a century ago. No one would ever mistake it for a spotless modern saltbox.

"I like it," Roland remarked, putting her fears to rest. "Clearly a house with a proper history. Lots of character."

Jacob chuckled. "That's one way of putting it, I guess.

Lots of shingles that have had to be replaced, and lots of layers of paint covering lots of—"

"Be quiet," Bailey snapped. "Our friend just complimented our home. No need to run the false modesty routine, Jacob."

"Whatever," he retorted. "I'm sure they've got places even older than this up in Seattle."

Roland nodded slowly. "They do. Some date back to around the time the Civil War ended, although that's nothing compared to some of the early English and Dutch places on the East Coast, or settlements established by the Spanish in Florida or the Southwest. The Northwest is still the wildest part of the contiguous United States."

Kurt made a stupid quip thanking him for the history lesson, of course, but something about his words had spoken deeply to them all.

Just as they were about to mount the front porch, the doors swung open and out stepped a small boy about seven years old. He was shirtless, barefoot, and dressed only in muddy jeans. He was lean but precociously muscular and had bright red hair and freckles.

He was also carrying a full-sized refrigerator on his back.

Roland jerked to a halt and then stumbled back a step, his eyes wide and his mouth open. "Holy *shit!*" he blurted.

The boy paid no attention to him. The bulky fridge had gotten stuck on the doorframe.

"Here," Bailey said, and she and Jacob sprang up the porch steps to help. They repositioned the appliance and floated some of its weight long enough for the kid to squeeze through, then they let go.

Jacob regarded the boy with a crooked but affectionate smile. "You got it?" he asked.

"Yup." The kid hitched the fridge up a notch, then thumped down the stairs, the huge white mass seeming to weigh no more than a backpack on his shoulders. "Hi, Kurt. Hi, Russell. Hey, who're you?"

Roland still seemed to be in shock, so Kurt spoke on his behalf. "His name's Roland. You might see him again later. Anyway, hope that thing works out for you."

"It will!" The boy beamed. "Thanks again. Bye!" He scampered off, the refrigerator bobbing and hiding him from sight after a moment, so it looked as though the appliance was floating by itself toward the house next door.

Roland rubbed his eyes. "The *hell*? What the fuck do you people put in the water around here, anabolic steroids? Those are illegal, you know, especially for a kid that age."

Bailey went to his side, biting her tongue as her brothers laughed at the out-of-towner's ignorance. "That's Joey Hauer, the neighbor boy," she told him. "He's a were-wolf. What you heard about this town is true. He could probably bench-press you a few times over."

The Seattleite's shock faded. His face now showed something like wonder.

"He's a sweet boy," Bailey went on. "A little rascally, but that's to be expected. He was just here to pick up a fridge that's getting replaced shortly. Literally pick up, I guess. Theirs broke, so—"

Kurt cut in. "At least he remembered to lift the damn thing door-side up. Otherwise, it might have fallen open, and we'd be picking the shelves up behind him."

Roland was still staring at the neighboring house, where Joey's family had emerged to help him finagle the appliance through their front door.

"Well, then," he marveled. "Werewolves do exist. And they're *that* strong? Incredible."

Bailey tried not to flush with pride. "I suppose it is, isn't it? And, well, we would know."

Roland turned and stared into her eyes.

This was it, Bailey realized. Time to come clean with him. There was no point in delaying any longer.

"All right," she announced, "let's go inside. Roland, we need to have a serious talk. About this town and the people in it. What you just saw proved that some of what you'd heard was true."

Her brothers eyed her, looking concerned, but for now, they didn't interrupt or protest.

Roland blew his breath out between his lips. "Yes, I think I'd like to have that talk. Seeing *that* freaked me out, but now I'm even more curious."

They all headed up the porch steps, and Jacob opened the front door.

"My friend," Kurt said, clapping the wizard on the back, "your curiosity is about to be satisfied."

They all filed in: Jacob, Russell, Bailey, Roland, and Kurt, in that order. The youngest brother pulled the door closed behind them.

The Nordin house's interior matched its exterior; it was old and old-fashioned but in reasonably good condition. Most of the furniture and appliances were unremarkable middle-class stuff that had been around at least a decade or two, but the place was clean and tasteful. It was slightly disorderly, what with boxes of junk in the corners, but Bailey would have been happy to say she wasn't embarrassed about the place.

Roland looked around, taking in the sights. Not passing judgment, just getting a feel for the location. He turned to Bailey.

"Are your parents home? Or anyone else?"

"Nah," she told him. "Dad's gone. He'll probably be back tomorrow. You want a glass of water or anything? Figure we might as well sit down. In the living room there would be good, or the kitchen table's fine."

Roland settled the issue by lowering himself onto the couch. "Water sounds good, thanks."

Bailey fetched him a glass, filling it from the kitchen sink. Since they didn't have a refrigerator right now, he'd just have to do without ice. The tap water came out cold enough.

She brought it out to the living room, where her brothers had already taken their own places—Jacob on the other end of the couch, Russell in the big leather easy chair, and Kurt reclining on the throw rug in front of the window.

The other Nordins were in the process of explaining further how things worked around here.

"The general attitude," Jacob extrapolated, "is that if we don't need something and one of our neighbors *does*, they ought to have it."

Kurt chimed in, "And vice versa, of course."

Bailey stepped into the midst of them. "Can it. We can discuss the local trade economy some other time." Roland looked interested in the subject, but he didn't protest. She handed him the glass.

The wizard accepted the water. "Thanks. Just occurred to me that I might need to use the bathroom soon."

"Yeah," Bailey remarked, "burn that bridge when you come to it. For now…"

She plopped down beside the wizard, wedging between him and Jacob. She waited for him to finish his first long sip before she started talking on the off chance he might spit his drink out.

Then she took a deep breath and began. "Roland, for all I know you already guessed, but we're werewolves, too. All of us. The entire Nordin family. So were those four assholes in the diner. And quite a few other people scattered throughout this valley, and some of the ones next door."

She paused awkwardly. She'd spoken almost too fast, like she was in a hurry to just blurt it out and get to the part where he reacted.

There was no denying it—she was nervous. She didn't want him to think badly of her or be weirded out to the point that he wouldn't know what to say and things would become all awkward.

She'd already offered to help him with what he seemed to think was a serious problem. He wouldn't reject that aid just because of what she was, would he? She wanted to squeeze her eyes shut but did not. She just swallowed the spit that had pooled under her tongue and waited to receive whatever the gods had decided was coming toward her.

Roland turned his body to match the position of his

face—toward her—and cocked his head at an angle, peering into her eyes. "Really? Well, that makes things even more interesting. I've never been personally acquainted with a werewolf, let alone a whole family of them."

Bailey laughed abruptly, mostly to disguise the expulsion of air that otherwise would have been an obvious sigh of relief. "They don't have many werewolves up by Seattle. I've heard of a few in Washington, but mostly way out in the boonies. Wild, unattached ones in the mountains and deep forests, supposedly."

The wizard shrugged. "I've heard rumors along those lines. Anyway, it's tempting for me to ask one of you to demonstrate by shifting into wolf form—"

Bailey's heart skipped a beat.

"—but if I did that," Roland went on, "it would only be fair for you to ask me to cast a spell or something. And I'd rather not, right now; the more obvious and visible magicks use up power I might need. Plus, it could potentially send out something like shockwaves or radio signals, which the fine ladies pursuing me might pick up on."

His face went grim at this with stoic anger. Bailey got a sense that he was already tired of dealing with the witches who were after him, and the breeding politics that had created the whole situation.

Again, Bailey felt a surge of warmth and empathy. She wanted to give him a hug, but that might be a bit much.

Kurt broke the pause. "Good on you," he complimented Roland, "for not being the judgmental type. Just gotta work on that whole 'seeing a kid lifting a fridge' startled reaction thing."

Russell nodded and added, "Yep."

Before Bailey could suggest they move on to discussing their plans for what to do with Roland in the meantime, Jacob beat her to it.

"Okay," he began, "so you can probably stick around for, I don't know, a couple days or something and just lie low, then we'll go from there. And we'll want to hear this grand idea of Bailey's."

The phone rang.

Bailey almost wanted to punch the wall at the interruption, but she restrained herself. Roland was closest to the phone, which sat on an end table next to the couch, but he wasn't about to answer someone else's landline, so Bailey stood up and handled it.

She picked up the receiver. "Hello?"

"Hi, Bailey," said a familiar voice. "It's Sheriff Browne up at the station. Say, did you bring that young gentleman back to your place? Everyone saw you walking out with him, so that seemed like a logical assumption."

Bailey turned her head and mouthed the word "fuck" into the air, making sure not to put any breath or volume behind it. Jacob saw her out of the corner of his eye but didn't interrupt.

She suddenly recalled the cop car that had driven past just before they'd had the powwow and turned down the side road toward her family's house. Trying to deny Roland was here would be useless and pointless. Besides, it was a small town, and everyone knew everyone else—including the police.

"Yeah," she responded, "he and my brothers are here, just talking and relaxing. Why do you ask, Sheriff?"

"Eh," he replied, in a drawling, casual tone, "curiosity.

Just wanted to make sure he's staying out of trouble. Seems one or two people complained about a disturbance at the diner, although I'm glad to hear things didn't get out of hand."

She was glad, too. "Yes, sir. Dan Oberlin was in a bad mood, but fortunately, he stopped at exchanging a few words, and my brothers and I did likewise."

By now, Roland and the male Nordins were listening in. Her brothers with their superior hearing could probably make out most or all of what Browne was saying. She wasn't sure about the wizard.

"Right," the sheriff went on. "Did you figure anything out, by chance? I mean, has our new friend explained in any more detail what he's doing here? I overheard him saying a few crazy-sounding things in the station, but that was probably just him trying to get a rise out of you."

Bailey retorted, "Just how he'd heard that Greenhearth was a nice little town, and it would get him away from…I think one of his exes is looking for him to start drama? Something like that. I'm not rightly sure."

Browne chuckled. "I suppose *maybe* I can believe that. You're sure you didn't just find him attractive enough that you brought him back home for some fun?"

Bailey stammered without making sound for a sec, but before she could protest, the sheriff cut back in.

"Just teasing you, ha-ha." He chuckled. Sometimes he got like that, mainly when talking to someone he knew well. He was all business when dealing with outsiders. "No need to take it personal."

She cleared her throat loudly. "Not the most polite thing you've ever said, even so."

"Don't mind me," the man's voice continued. "Anyhow, just curious how things were going. And if that guy Roland leaves nice and soon, and doesn't cause any problems until he does, we can forget all about the minor speeding."

Bailey grimaced. She had been under the impression that he'd been released with a warning or otherwise cleared of that nonsense. Obviously something else was going on right now.

"Why are you being so nice, Sheriff? Is there something you want to know? Might as well just ask if that's the case." Her tone had just enough edge for him to get the point without making it seem like she was giving him lip.

There was a pause on the other end of the line. "Like I said, I have a good nose for trouble, and I do believe trouble has come to town."

Glancing up, Bailey saw her brothers, who must have overheard, eyeing Roland. For his part, the wizard just sat there calmly, a neutral expression on his face.

Browne couldn't have been talking about Roland. He'd already released him.

She returned her attention to the phone. "Who or what are you talking about, sir?"

"Three women," the sheriff said at once. "They just rolled into town in a convertible—real attractive ladies, classy-like, probably from the city. You can smell the money on them. As it happens, they're looking for someone meeting the description of your boy there."

Bailey's stomach tightened up and went cold. "I see. Could you, uh, hold on a sec?"

"Certainly."

She covered the receiver with her hand and turned to

Roland. "Bad news," she said softly. He raised his eyebrows, and Bailey repeated to him everything the sheriff had just told her.

Roland tilted his head far back and almost slapped himself in the face as he covered his eyes with his hand. "Goddammit," he grated. "I mean, I suppose it could technically be some other trio of swanky ladies in a convertible."

He leaned forward and looked at Bailey. "Ask him to describe the vehicle."

Nodding, the girl removed her hand and spoke into the receiver. "Uh, Sheriff, could you describe the car they are driving?"

"Sure thing," Browne agreed. There was a brief delay, accompanied by a heavy sigh and some shuffling sounds, as though he'd written down the details and already lost it amidst the other papers on his desk.

Bailey's tapped her fingers on the end table in her impatience.

"Let's see," the man continued. "It's a silver 2011 Jaguar XKR, four-seater, two-door. Nice car if I may say so. Does that ring a bell?"

"Hold on." Again, Bailey hand-muted the phone and relayed the information to Roland.

He shook his head, frowning with something more like annoyance than fear, yet she could sense the subtle tension that had spread through his whole body. He was trying to keep himself under control.

He sighed. "Well, that would be *them.*"

Kurt added his two cents. "Shit. Well, no offense, but if they're witches, you kinda had to figure they'd have a few tricks up their sleeves for finding people they're looking for. Right?"

Roland nodded. "I *did* figure, but they're better than I gave them credit for."

Bailey waved her arm sharply at them. "Pipe down. We can discuss this after I'm done talking to the sheriff."

Once they shut up, she resumed her conversation. "Thank you, Sheriff. We'll keep that in mind. And don't worry; no one wants any trouble."

Browne coughed. "They sure seem to," he muttered. "Annoying rich chicks, acting all entitled and like us country bumpkins don't have a right to stand between them and whatever it is they want. Pretty clear they've got an agenda of some kind involving our man Roland. Again, I don't want any ugliness here."

Before Bailey could respond, she heard noise in the background, although it was hard to make out. Human voices—female voices—seemed to be involved, though.

Then the sheriff resumed speaking, now at a much louder volume. "So, then," he practically shouted into the phone, "do you have any idea where this Roland guy is?"

For a split second, Bailey was confused, but then it struck her. The man had just asked that for show. His three visitors were meant to overhear it, and it was supposed to provide her with a certain amount of cover.

"Uh," Bailey stammered, "well, no, not really, Sheriff. We'll keep you posted if he does turn up."

"You do that," Browne urged. "I'll let you go for now. Have a nice day."

The voices in the background piped up again and seemed to be moving closer to the phone.

"You too," said Bailey. She hung up and turned to the four men.

Jacob spread his hands. "Well?"

"Well," she shot back, "we've got some talking to do and some plans to make."

***

For whatever reason, the living room, and the house in general, had started to feel stuffy, almost oppressive. The rain seemed to have let up for the rest of the day, or at least for a couple more hours, so they'd wandered out back, strolling around the Nordin property as they discussed what to do next.

The backyard was a mixture of grass and mud. There was a moldering, moss-covered woodpile at the far rear corner of the lot, composed mostly of branches they'd trimmed in the surrounding pine forest to keep the trees from shrinking the property with their encroachment.

They also had a pole barn back and center of the yard, which was beginning to rust around the edges. They kept their lawn tractor and most of their tools in there, and it was where Bailey and Jacob did most of their tinkering with half-viable automobiles. Sometimes fully viable ones.

Jacob grunted. "At least we know what kind of vehicle to look for in case they start cruising around for their victim. Silver Jaguar. Not a lot of those around here, so they ought to stick out like a sore thumb."

"Ugh," Roland assented, "yes. And let me tell you something. Those three might be driving a Jaguar, but they're a nasty enough bunch that in another ten years, they'll all be cougars."

All three of the Nordin males burst out laughing at that. Jacob guffawed, hands on his stomach. Kurt cackled and slapped his knee, and even Russell turned his head down and chuckled while shaking his head.

Bailey laughed, too, partially because her brothers' mirth was contagious, and partly because it was good to know that Roland had a sense of humor.

Yet, just knowing the witches were in town put a damper on the moment. Somehow, Roland's comment had just served to emphasize the danger he was in. Bailey didn't know much about witchcraft or wizardry. What would they be able to do to him?

For that matter, she wondered, what would they be able to do to her and her family if they decided to punish them for helping Roland?

Her brothers must have picked up on the vibe and reached the same conclusion since they sobered up from their laughing fit pretty quick. By now, they'd trudged halfway across the yard, trying to keep to the less-muddy areas. That was for Roland's sake since the Nordins didn't care. Bailey figured they'd end up in the pole barn.

Bailey let out a small snort. "You know," she commented, "if these goddamn witches are already here, and assuming they have, you know, powers of persuasion beyond what any decent-looking woman has, it's not gonna be long before they start talking to people and asking around. They're probably gonna get just the answers they want."

Roland gave her a halfhearted thumbs-up. "I'd say that's

an accurate assessment. You don't happen to have an abandoned fruit cellar or something you could hide me in? Or maybe a commando tunnel dug through the ground under the woods over there?"

Kurt chuckled. "Not quite. Digging one of those might be fun, though. Thanks for the idea. We'd just have to get the weight calculations right so the whole thing didn't collapse on us."

"Cute," Jacob grumbled. "Thanks, Kurt. We'll keep that in mind."

Kurt smirked. "Don't mention it."

The oldest of the brothers turned to the newcomer. "Roland, my friend, I'm thinking you can't stay here. Even if we did have a fruit cellar or a frickin' tunnel, I don't think it would keep you hidden for long."

Roland frowned. Bailey, hovering beside him, could tell that he knew this, and had known it even before Jacob had said it, but he was trying to avoid having to reach the conclusion.

Jacob added, "Don't get me wrong. Not saying that because we want to get rid of you. You're all right, actually. I just mean, realistically, if they know basically where you are, then your chances aren't good."

"Dammit!" Bailey interjected. "We can't just send him on his merry way again. That won't solve anything, and he'll just end up running away until he hits Boston or Miami or something. Then what the hell's he gonna do?"

Roland sighed. "Good question."

As Bailey had predicted, their little group found its way to the side door of the pole barn. Russell, having the longest legs and all, had outpaced the others and gotten out in front, and he opened the door, ducked in, and held it for the rest of them as they filed in.

Bailey flipped on the light. The overhead fluorescents flickered for a moment and then buzzed to life, flooding the space with bright white illumination. It was merciless in revealing the general dirtiness and disarray of the place, but then again, a pole barn wasn't the same thing as a living room.

In the center of the building was a 2006 black Toyota Tundra. It was lifted, not to a ridiculous degree, but enough to look cool. Just enough that you could tell it had been modified by someone who knew what they were doing.

"Bailey," Jacob asked, "did you ever get that thing running again?" He gestured to the truck.

Bailey grinned. "Yessir." She didn't try to hide the pride in her voice, and she could feel her brother's pride in her.

Roland rubbed his chin as he examined the vehicle. "Not bad. What was wrong with it?"

"Tell you later," said Bailey. "You know, I'm thinking maybe we need to get out of town-town. I mean, we're kinda on the edge here, but Main Street isn't far. Our friend from Seattle will be safer out in the country, I'm thinking."

Russell glowered, already calculating the risks. "How far out are we talking?"

"Probably," Bailey began, "one of the old farms to the northeast. That'll take us out of town and also away from South Cliff territory, just in case *those* dipshits end up getting involved."

The brothers nodded slowly. They did not miss the

implications of Bailey's choice of words: us. She didn't intend to send the wizard off by himself.

Meanwhile, Roland kept silent. He clearly trusted their judgment and had until further notice placed himself in their capable hands. He was apparently smart enough to grasp that the Nordins knew the countryside around here a lot better than he did. He wasn't about to queer things by asking what they were getting out of it. He figured he'd find out sooner or later, and they seemed like good people.

Jacob scowled. "Bailey, you're a grown woman and all, but Dad's still going get worried as hell if you're gone too long. We can stall him for a little while, but you ought to come back after a day or two, at least to check in. Don't forget about Gunney, either."

The girl smiled. "I won't. Just tell Dad I needed a vacation. Too many assholes around lately."

Roland cracked his knuckles. "I can agree with that. Just one question, though..." His voice trailed off, and he waited till he had their attention. "How will we get to one of those old farms?"

Half of Bailey's smile returned, and she playfully prodded the wizard's foot with her boot. Then she gestured to the center of the pole barn with her elbow.

"How the hell do you think?"

CHAPTER SIX

The truck careened down the bumpy, rutted, quasi-paved road. It left mud tracks on the patches of decades-old asphalt and then picked up more mud when it hit an unpaved section.

Bailey glanced at her passenger with a barely suppressed smirk on her face. "You ever been this high up in a vehicle before?" she inquired.

Roland seemed to mostly be enjoying the bumpy ride. His face was often broken by a goofy, crooked smile, or he'd laugh and say "Whoa!" when they went down a slope too fast and got that special feeling in the pits of their stomachs. He did brace himself against the seat whenever they hit a particularly large bump, though.

"Well," he responded, his hair flipping over as the vehicle rocked in time with his turning toward her, "I do seem to recall being on a school bus a few times as a kid."

"Hah!" Bailey scoffed. "They can't get away with driving like this. Don't you worry. I know what I'm doing, and I know what this vehicle is capable of since I practically built the damn thing. It's one of my babies."

"*One of?*" Roland repeated. "The other one isn't a poodle, is it?"

"Hell, no!" She decided not to be offended since it was obviously a joke. It probably hadn't occurred to him that Weres did not keep dogs as pets on general principles.

Instead, she stuck to the subject at hand. "I'll tell you about the rest of my babies some other time. As for the Tundra here, I bought it used and in pretty shitty condition just over a year ago. Ever since then, working on it off and on has been a project of mine. Now, when I first looked under the hood…"

She went on to describe in detail all the problems the vehicle had suffered from—busted engine parts, weak tie rods, a coolant leak, old-ass tires, and a rusted bed—and all the labor she'd put in to get it up to speed, in fact making it better than it had been when new.

The wizard didn't understand all the technical details since he wasn't a car person, but he listened anyway. "Interesting." he opined.

To her delight, Bailey concluded that Roland hadn't just said that to fill in the gaps in the conversation. He truly, legitimately *did* find it interesting. He seemed curious about things in general, and he listened to her when she spoke.

He went on, "Where I come from, most people only have trucks if they really like them—fanboys, collectors, and the like, mainly—or if they need them for labor purposes. Like if they're a contractor and need a flatbed to load all of their construction materials or lawn care tools or whatever. Professional purposes. No one drives a truck simply because they think it's practical." He shrugged.

"Weirdos." Bailey chuckled. "I guess the land up there is mostly flat, and all the roads are paved."

"Mostly." Roland sighed. "Although some of the less-popular streets have potholes that I'm pretty sure would swallow even this thing," he gestured around them, "without a trace. They'd have to send in a team of professional spelunkers just to *find* it."

Bailey snickered at that. "Your tax dollars at work."

Silence set in, but it was an easy, comfortable silence. For a couple of minutes, they were content just to drive, the road now heading back uphill as they pushed deeper into the foothills. The afternoon was growing warmer, and they rolled down the windows.

Roland leaned back and let the cool, damp breeze blow his straw-colored hair back from his face. "I have to admit," he began, "I'm pretty damn curious to see what it will be like to spend time on an actual farm."

Bailey turned to him, squinting with mock surprise and disapproval. "You've never even *been* on a farm before? For shame!"

He just shrugged. "Seattle is a big city, and once you get outside the city-city, you're in the suburbs. Those might be more spread out and with fewer tall buildings, but they're no less developed. And then you're back in an urban environment, more or less, as you head south into Tacoma, and then more suburbs until you're in Olympia."

Bailey shook her head slowly. Her brain could grasp the idea of a metropolitan area that stretched for miles and miles, but she'd never seen one, been in one, or had to navigate one. Greenhearth was just Greenhearth, and then there were the rustic outskirts, the forest, and the mountains. That was all.

"So," the wizard went on, "farms are mostly a concept to me. The way death and the solar system are concepts. People are aware of them, but no one has the first-hand experience to say they know such things the way they know their own neighborhood or a game they've beaten eight times or a job they had for ten years."

Bailey burst out laughing. "I was just thinking the same thing about cities. Like, I can kinda picture what you're talking about, but I'd have to see one firsthand to get a feel for it."

Roland smiled and gave her an appreciative nod. "In that, you might say we have something in common, precisely because of what we *don't* have in common. If that makes sense."

"It does," she acceded. "Everybody has their own story, even if it's a different story."

"Right." He ran a hand through his hair, and she suddenly wished the sun was shining to emphasize its gold hue. "I'm sure somewhere in the Brazilian rainforest or on the Mongolian steppe, there's someone to whom even Greenhearth, Oregon, would seem like a bustling, ultramodern metropolis."

"Well," Bailey quipped, "wouldn't *that* just be the nicest compliment ever. Of course, to someone like that, Seattle might, I dunno, kill them."

Roland sighed. "The traffic probably would, yeah."

The wizard reclined in his seat, and something about his

energy changed. It was difficult to describe, but Bailey picked up on it nonetheless, a product of both her female intuition and her advanced senses as a Were. He was preparing to say something that, until now, he'd been holding back.

"I wasn't sure if I should even talk about this," he began, instantly confirming her suspicion, "but, well, I feel like we have a good, easy rapport by now. I don't have an agenda or ulterior motive in saying this. It's just something I'd like to get off my chest."

Bailey shot him a glance before returning her attention to the road. They were bumping through a winding, somewhat difficult stretch of hillside forest that acted as the final challenge before the relatively flat land of the old farm. She hoped she looked open and sympathetic since she wanted him to go on.

He did. "So, I might have been putting on a tough façade, trying to act confident and like everything is no big deal. It's true that I can handle myself most of the time, but I'm honestly uneasy as hell with this situation."

The girl's gut clenched. Just when she felt like things were good with him, he had to go and drop a bombshell like *that*. Before she could ask him to clarify what he meant, though, he continued.

"I'm being *hunted*," he stated. "For my body, like an animal being chased down for meat. There's something inherently unsettling about that, no matter how you slice the details."

Bailey relaxed at once. He meant the broader situation involving the three witches, not the immediate one involving her.

"When you put it like that," she agreed, "it *does* sound pretty damn bad."

"Yes," he said. "And this isn't a new thing, either. I'm tired—really, truly sick and tired—of being pursued by people like them who just want to use me as a sex toy or a sperm dispenser. Oh, yes, ha-ha, I've heard all the jokes, like what those two guys at the sheriff's station were saying, or your brother after that, no offense to him. But it's not like that. Most people can't understand."

She nodded, waiting for him to go on with his story.

He sighed again, this time deeper and lower—a sound born of years of exasperation and disappointment.

"I just wish it was possible to meet people under normal circumstances and find someone who likes me for me, wizard status and all that magical power bullshit notwithstanding. To get to know someone and have things grow organically with them, not just be treated like a prize racehorse everyone wants to purchase or steal."

Listening to him speak, Bailey's stomach tightened once more, but this time it was different. Everything Roland had just said had struck a nerve. For a brief instant, she wanted to wrap her arms around him and tell him that she understood and that everything would be okay.

But she still had to drive. They were near the end of the winding forest path.

Roland waved a hand slowly. "So, I don't know; maybe it doesn't make much sense. As I've gotten older, I've learned more about the way regular people live, and sometimes I envy them, to be honest."

Bailey said, forcefully but with warmth, "You don't have

to say that or apologize or anything. It *does* make sense, believe me."

The man turned his head toward her, tilting it at an angle and almost staring at her. "Does it? That's a pleasant surprise, if so."

"Yeah," she assured him. "And I'm happy to surprise you, even if my reasons aren't all that pleasant."

He rubbed his chin with his fingers. "I see. Something to do with, well, being a werewolf?"

She nodded fiercely. "That would be it. There's more to it than you know. You heard some of the crap Dan Oberlin was saying about me scaring off potential mates and all that?"

Roland sat back in his seat as they emerged from the woods into a small valley where tall grass covered most of the open land.

"I did hear that," he confirmed.

"Well," Bailey explained, "that wasn't just him being a loudmouthed no-account Cro Magnon bastard, as sorry as I am to have to say that. We—our people—have, y'know, our own rules and traditions and things like that, especially governing marriage. And breeding. And most of those fall harder on the women."

He frowned. "I see. You can tell me about it if you want."

She did want to. In fact, she'd wanted to be able to vent about it, to spill the beans to someone—anyone—who didn't have a preconceived opinion on the matter. That was a luxury she hadn't had anytime recently, if ever.

"According to the all-important pack laws," she went on, "all females have to be married by the age of twenty-five. If we haven't already found a mate—husband—by that time, we get the arranged marriage treatment and are hooked up with whoever's considered the best available bachelor at the next all-packs gathering.

"Well, I'm twenty-four and some change, and my birthday isn't too far away. I ain't exactly looking forward to it. Don't know whether to shit or go blind, as Gunney would say."

Roland's serious demeanor cracked, and he snickered at the last bit. "Sorry," he added quickly, "I just never heard that particular colorful expression before. Not laughing at your plight. If anything, well, it sounds a little too familiar."

Bailey allowed her face to settle into a mild, gentle smile. "I knew you weren't laughing at me. This doesn't apply to the males, by the way. There are ways they can get out of it. I'll tell you about that another time."

"Yeah, okay. Who's Gunney, anyway? Hopefully, I'll get to meet him before this is all over," Roland suggested.

Bailey thought that sounded pretty ominous, but she tried to ignore it. "Hopefully, you will. Gunney's my boss at the auto shop. Honestly, he's almost like a second father. He's full of what you would call 'colorful expressions.' You might like him. Anyhow, all of a sudden, I'm wondering. Like, there are people who will pursue someone they want no matter what, but generally, a person gets left alone more if they're, you know, *taken*."

Roland's brow furrowed as her words sunk in. So this was what she would get out of it. He'd hoped she'd get to it sooner rather than later.

She pressed on. "Or at least, if everyone *thinks* that they're already taken. So, um, to put it bluntly," she drew a breath, suddenly nervous about how he might react, "I wonder if it might help, y'know, alleviate both our problems if I pretended to be your girlfriend?"

Silence followed her suggestion, and the following seconds seemed to last for minutes each. They were almost to the farm now and she slowed down, trying to breathe normally.

"Huh," Roland mused. "That's…actually a pretty goddamn clever idea."

Bailey's eyes closed of their own will in relief, but she made herself open them again right away so as not to be too obvious about it. She didn't want him to think she was desperate or anything.

The wizard continued, "I mean, it's no guarantee. These women who are after me won't care, although it might give them pause. Still, they're ruthless enough to consider any girlfriend I might have illegitimate, as just an obstacle for them to sweep aside. That Oberlin prick doesn't seem much better. But it's worth a shot. It ought to at least shut everyone else up—the people who *aren't* psychopaths but aren't helping, either."

"Yeah," Bailey agreed. "It's worth a shot. Besides, it might be fun." The mischievous grin crept back onto her face.

Roland matched the expression, to her pleased surprise. "I can agree with that. It's been so long since I've had a girlfriend. It seems like I've spent years dodging magically empowered insane bimbos, which really gets in the way of going on dates. At this point, even having a *pretend* girlfriend ought to be nice."

They rolled up the front drive of the farm.

"Yeah," Bailey said. "I think it will be."

The farm had originally belonged to one of Bailey's great-uncles, and the family still owned the land. The old man's children had neither the taste nor the talent for agriculture, so after he'd passed away, there had been no one to take his place. The farmhouse sat vacant while the fields went fallow and began to return to the wilderness from which they'd been carved.

The house was light blue with a roof of black shingles, although the paint was peeling in places and some of the shingles had fallen off. About once a month, the Nordin kids would visit and do some cursory sweeping-out of the house's interior just to keep it from becoming too filthy, but no one had the time, energy, or inclination to make it livable again.

Back a few hundred feet from the house was a big red barn. It wasn't a pole barn like Bailey's, but full-sized—the real deal. It also looked dilapidated, but it was so sturdily built that the years had not compromised its basic integrity. It might stand for decades yet.

Bailey wheeled the truck around the house to the side and parked in the muddy lot out back, so the vehicle would not be immediately visible on the off chance someone came down the road and scoped out the property.

Of course, there was still the matter of the fresh tire tracks in the mud, but she couldn't do much about those unless she felt like smoothing out half a mile's worth of road with a shovel.

"Well," she announced as she shifted into park and killed the engine, "we're here."

Roland smiled and nodded. "Home sweet home, for now. Pardon my asking, but does this place have things like heat and electricity and running water?"

His companion grimaced. "Shit. No, it doesn't. Probably should've thought of that." She exhaled and tried not to be angry with herself.

Instead, she turned her mind to practical solutions. "We'll make do, though. Ought to be fine for the rest of the day, at least, and under cover of night, I can sneak back home or into town and get us some bottled water, a kerosene heater, battery-powered lights, and all that good stuff."

Roland unbuckled his seat belt and shrugged. "That's a start. Not sure I—we—will be able to live like that indefinitely, but if we're lucky, it will suffice for a few days while we hide from both of our groups of unwanted suitors."

They both opened the doors of the cab and stepped out, inhaling the fresh air and feeling the earth beneath their feet. Roland wasn't dressed "country," and he wore shoes rather than boots, but his wardrobe was casual enough to get by. He didn't seem too bothered by the mud.

Bailey gestured past the house. "Let's go into the barn," she offered. "More space than the house, and besides, I want to check how it's doing in there. My family still owns this property, but it doesn't get much attention anymore."

"Okay," Roland agreed.

They walked across the faint dirt track that was all that remained of the path leading from house to barn amidst the wild grasses and shrubs that were steadily reclaiming the land. Examining the sky, Bailey noticed that the clouds were gone now. They were nearing the transition from early to mid-afternoon; several hours of sunlight remained, but sunset wasn't too far off.

They reached the large sliding double wooden doors that led into the barn's interior, with boards crossing their fronts in the shape of an X. Bailey seized the left one and heaved it to the side. It groaned and creaked but cooperated with her efforts.

Seeing that she didn't need help, Roland grabbed the right door and pushed. It budged slightly, and he grunted and threw himself against it. Then it started to slide, and he stopped when it was halfway open, deciding he'd done enough.

Bailey looked at him, having opened her side all the way with a single motion. "We really only needed to open the one, you know," she pointed out, "but thanks. Oh, and don't beat yourself up. Those doors are heavy. I'm, you know, stronger than most people. Always have been."

Roland raised his eyebrows. "Looks like it. I was kinda hoping the right door was just heavier or stuck on something. It's good to know that you can bench-press a refrigerator. Wait, shit! That *kid* could lift a fridge, so you could probably bench press your frickin' *truck*."

She chuckled at the thought. "You know, I haven't tried, but I might be able to. I just might."

They strolled in, and Bailey casually pulled both the doors shut behind them. A few high windows let in enough light for them to see where they were going, but mostly the barn lay in deep gloom. It smelled moldy and musty, but not terrible, and this time of year, there weren't likely to be bugs or spiders around.

Bailey turned to look at her new pseudo-boyfriend. "Right, so," she began, "I figure the first thing we need to do is come up with an action plan for getting around the area without being too direct about it. Don't want to drive straight through town if we can help it."

Roland was absorbed in looking around for a place to sit or lean comfortably, but he was listening to her.

"Sounds like a good idea," he remarked. "There'd be more chance of them seeing us if we did that, especially in such a small community. Not to mention they're probably using somewhere in the middle of town as their base of operations, so any trace we leave there could easily be picked up by any tracking magic they might employ. Which is a real possibility, by the way. There's three of them, so a tiring magical operation would still leave the other two to pick up the slack."

That was a disturbing notion, Bailey decided. She hadn't thought of it that way, but it was true. Even if Roland was more powerful than usual for a wizard, he was only one man.

She flipped her brown hair over her shoulder and put her hands on her hips. "Yeah, definitely. In fact, now that I think about it, it might be better if I went and got us the supplies sooner rather than later. The witches won't have had as much time to look around and talk to people."

"Right," the Seattleite assented. "Also, do you have a map? I did scope this place out on Google, but it seems like some of the back roads and, uh, goat trails or whatever some of these don't appear on the app. Just the major streets. It would be helpful to know all the byways and shortcuts and long scenic routes in case I have to make a hasty getaway on my own."

Bailey nodded, although she didn't like the thought of him fleeing without her. She told herself he was probably just thinking of her safety—of situations where he didn't want her involved with whatever trouble might be crashing toward them.

But as far as she was concerned, they were in this together now. And they would stick together, just as if they were boyfriend and girlfriend for real.

"I don't," she stated, "anticipate that becoming an issue. But I understand what you mean. Pull up Google Maps, then, and I can at least point out to you where the 'goat trails' are in relation to however much they show on there. We can try satellite view."

He did, cursing the slow and uncertain connection this far out in the sticks. Still, the app loaded after a couple of minutes, and he zoomed it, so it showed Greenhearth's layout with a fair degree of detail, with some of the surrounding countryside visible as well.

"Mmkay," Bailey began, "we're right about here. The dirt road leading to the farm isn't listed, I see. There's another dirt road out back—I'll show you a little later— that leads up this way through some rough country," she indicated where with her pinky finger, "and it intersects with Spruce Road right here, which then goes back to Main about a mile east of town. That will be our rear escape avenue."

He nodded. "Good. What else?"

They spent a few more minutes hashing out directions

and fallback plans. Roland seemed satisfied, maybe even impressed with the depth and usefulness of her local knowledge.

"And this is the route I'm gonna take to get supplies," she said. "As for going back to our house, there's only the one route, so we'll just have to hope and pray in that case."

"Right." He rubbed his eyes; staring at the small, lighted screen in the shadowy barn was straining them. "Sometimes that's all you can do."

He tapped out of Maps and pocketed his phone, then seemed to rest for a moment. He was getting tired, she figured—mentally more than physically. Still, he gave off an electrical signal she found strangely appealing.

"So," she queried, keeping her tone as casual as she could, "I take it your three wannabe baby-mamas aren't your type?"

He almost squirmed in discomfort. "Correct, they're not. Even if they weren't trying to practically stick me in a tube and hook a tap to my balls, I wouldn't want anything to do with them. They're like those chicks on *Sex and the City*. Ugh."

Bailey chortled at that. She didn't watch that show, but she got his drift. "I see. So, what would you say *is* your type? I mean, just, you know… What kind of people do you like?" She cleared her throat. "In general."

Roland found a sufficiently non-cobwebbed patch of wall and leaned against it, raising his right leg to lay his foot flat against the wood.

"Hmm," he mused. "I don't pay much attention to the superficial stuff. Of course, every man notices when a girl is attractive in general, but looks aren't all-important.

Appearances can be bought, and like the saying goes, they can be deceiving."

Bailey nodded. She sometimes wore makeup, but only a little.

Roland continued his spiel. "I guess you could say that I like girls—people, really—who are tough and 'real.' Not in the sense of being mindlessly aggressive or whatever, but people who can hold their own and get things done. Wizards and witches have gotten too reliant on magic and status and tradition and appearances over the years. There's something refreshing about people who don't mind getting their hands dirty."

Softly, Bailey responded, "You've come to the right place, then."

He smiled. "Kinda seems like it, doesn't it? I've been dealing with airhead bimbos my whole life. People who are chasing the image they want to project to the world. I'm through with that shit, though. I mean, I got a lot of attention, and I liked it at first, as a kid. Who wouldn't?"

Suddenly Bailey found herself wondering how many girls he'd been with. It wasn't technically any of her business, but her brain couldn't keep itself from asking the question.

"But," he went on, "some time ago, I figured out that I was just a *commodity* to those people. Every girl or young woman I met who was a witch acted like I was a walking mass of candy. Not trying to brag, but for people with sufficient magical sensitivity, I give off an aura of power they seem to find irresistible."

There was something about him, Bailey had to admit.

"And as for the normal girls," he continued, running a

hand through his hair, "they noticed the witches wanting me, so they wanted me, too. You know how females are, no offense. I was drunk on always being wanted by the time I was nine years old."

Bailey blinked and almost fell back a step. "Nine? They weren't, you know…"

He gave her a sad half-smile, half-grimace. "The sexual overtures didn't start till a few years later, but I guess you could say the groundwork was laid in childhood. If I was drunk on the attention at nine, I was hungover by fifteen. I have spent the rest of my time as more or less a hermit, interacting as little as possible. Now I'd rather just sober up."

She took a moment to ponder his words, to digest them. Then she folded her arms over her chest. "Roland my friend, it sounds like you've led an interesting life, I'll say that much. Shit, you got some balls, having finally just run away. Are you trying to start over? I almost wish I could do the same thing."

He spread his hands. "I'm not sure yet. I've missed a lot in life. At the very least, I need a long vacation away from Seattle, from the magical community, and from everyone I've ever known. I'd like to see more of the country, maybe go on a vision quest or something. Possibly I'll go back when the coast is clear, or I won't. I kinda like it here, though. There aren't people like you where I'm from."

At that, something fluttered in Bailey's stomach.

Before she could respond, she picked up the sounds of people—at least four—moving heavily toward the barn.

She almost slapped herself in the face. She'd been so engrossed in Roland's story that she hadn't noticed what should have been obvious to her much sooner. Quickly she pivoted toward the doors.

There was a crash and the cracking of wood, and the right-side barn door flew inwards, bent in the middle and nearly broken in two, disclosing a square patch of light that was partially blocked by a cluster of hulking figures.

Bailey recognized them immediately. She'd known who it was even before she'd seen them.

A familiar voice growled, "Well, well, well. We happened to be in the neighborhood, and look who we stumbled across."

Dan Oberlin grinned at his own wit, his beard bristling around his lips and teeth. His cronies mimicked the expression. In addition to the three who'd been with him at the diner, he'd picked up another South Cliff scumbag somewhere along the way.

By now, Bailey had positioned herself to where she could clearly see them, but she was partially protected by one of the wooden posts holding up the loft. Roland had come up just behind and to the side of her.

Bailey snorted. "The *neighborhood?*" She looked around as if in wonderment. "There's nothing around here but trees, shrubs, mud, and random small animals. Just how many wrong turns did you dipshits manage to take?"

Roland bit his tongue and turned his face to the ground, but she could still hear the sudden expulsion of air from his nose as he tried not to laugh.

Glowering at her, Oberlin flexed his big hands. "Enough to see that there's a bitch in the woods who needs a little training."

The Nordin brothers weren't around to restrain their

sister this time, but then again, they weren't in the diner anymore, either. No civilians, no witnesses. That made a big difference.

Although Bailey could already feel the red haze of anger creeping over her brain, she restrained herself for the moment. Five Weres might be a bit much, even for her. She had no idea how well Roland could handle himself in a fight.

"Y'know," she shot back at the gang, "I should have figured that stink was you guys. At first, I thought my truck was running rich, but then I remembered that it never has issues. Why the fuck are you here?"

She glanced at Roland to see how he was doing. He was looking at her, and his face was scrunched in confusion. *"Running rich?"* he asked.

"I'll tell you later," she replied quickly, then turned back to Dan and his pals.

All the mirth had drained from Oberlin's square face. "Cut the bullshit. We followed you. I figured I'd give you another chance to be mine."

Bailey met his stare, fists planted on her hips. "Marriage doesn't agree with me," she said flatly.

"Fuck marriage!" Dan raged. "We don't need to bother with that. Just hook up with me; that's all you gotta do. It'll get your folks and your pack off your back, and I'll get the same benefit. We'll be mated, and that will be good enough for everyone."

She continued to glare at him, not even blinking, while Roland tried not to barge into the conversation. The wizard seemed almost shocked. By now, Bailey had figured out that other groups of people had much different views on mating than the more degenerate sorts of werewolves did.

But she said nothing.

Oberlin's seething anger grew. "And if not," he continued, shrugging and baring his teeth, "I guess you'll just be another stupid bitch I put in her place. Can't let that public disrespect from earlier slide."

His boys chuckled, apparently basking in the machismo of their glorious leader.

None of them seemed to notice, though, that a switch had just flipped in Bailey's mind. Calling her that once had been bad enough, but Dan had done it twice in as many minutes. As far as she was concerned, he was already hooked up to an IV tube in intensive care.

Before she leaped into action, though, one of Dan's minions—the squat, multi-chinned guy Russell had nearly dismantled back at the diner—gestured contemptuously at Roland.

"Who's this scrawny fuck, anyway?"

Roland stepped forward, speaking for himself. "I'm her boyfriend," he stated, his tone even but firm. He turned his glance from Chins to Oberlin. "And I really don't think you should have called her a bitch. Twice, even. That was excessive."

Dan snorted so loudly that Bailey was amazed snot didn't shoot out of his nose. "And why the hell is that?"

"Because," the wizard said in the same steely, matter-of-fact voice, "I'm about to kick your ass."

CHAPTER SEVEN

All hell broke loose. Just before Bailey dropped the last of her inhibitions like a scalding pan and tackled Dan Oberlin head-on, she saw that, oddly, Roland was undoing his belt and pulling it out of the loops on his jeans.

"Get her!" one of the South Cliffs barked. Bodies moved and tangled in the irregular light in front of the barn entrance.

Bailey crashed into Dan's waist, her arms clamping around his midsection to lift him off the ground even as one of his boots kicked at her leg and his arms clamped down on her. His foot struck her shin, but at an angle that caused the blow to glance off. It might be bruised later, but nothing serious.

"Goddammit!" Oberlin snarled. His hands twisted into her hair and the fabric of her shirt around the shoulders, but she'd already heaved him up and back, throwing him toward the left doorframe. His left hand released her hair, but his right took a small piece of her shirt with it.

It was worth it, though, because he smashed into the

door, splintering the wood down the middle and then tumbling aside to land on his ass in the muddy yard. His legs were sticking straight up into the air.

Then she plunged toward the guy behind him, teeth bared and fists flying.

Meanwhile, Chins had made a beeline for the out-of-towner.

The freed belt snapped up and out like a whip. It looked at first as though Roland had swung it toward the tubby man's voluminous midsection, but its end somehow shot upward mid-strike to lash across his face.

"Shit!" Chins cried out in pain, his momentum halted as his hands reflexively went up to his jaw and mouth and lower cheek, where a nasty red welt was already forming. His lips split and swelled up even as they bled.

Then Roland snapped the belt again, this time lower, and it wrapped around the man's calf. The wizard gave a short, sharp tug and Chins' feet flew out from under him, sending him crashing into the fallen remains of the right-side barn door. He lay there, groaning.

Bailey was now taking on two of the South Cliffs at once as Dan Oberlin struggled back to his feet. Another of the South Cliffs was trying to help encircle Bailey, while the last of them was closing in on Roland.

For his part, the wizard had advanced to the threshold, trying to be near his supposed girlfriend as the fight worked its way outdoors.

Bailey was just about to deck the gangly bastard in front of her when one of the others pounced on her from behind, wrapping a thick, sweaty arm around her neck. Unfortunately for him, his hand ended up near her mouth.

She put her chin down and bit hard into the meat near the base of Sweaty's thumb. As he let out a ragged yell of pain, Gangly moved in on Bailey.

The girl surprised him by jumping up, still in the other man's grip, and kicking both legs square into his midsection. He let out an *oof* that indicated the wind had been knocked from his lungs, but as he doubled over, the noise turned into more of a gurgle. He fell to his knees and heaved, trying not to puke.

Bailey jerked up Sweaty's arm and he cooperated, just trying to free his hand from her teeth. The instant she released it, his fist lashed out at her torso while her fist drove toward his face.

Both found their mark. Bailey's knuckles connected with the bastard's nose, squashing it and drawing blood, and his balled-up hand bludgeoned her in the side, missing her kidney by an inch or two. They stumbled away from each other.

Sweaty's leg then came up clumsily, his shin hitting the back of Bailey's knee. Not hard enough to damage it, but enough to force the knee to bend, dropping her halfway to the ground.

She was already anticipating the next move. Sweaty, his face livid with incoherent anger, raised his foot for a stomp-kick to her face, she seized his foot and pulled straight up. With the momentum of the kick, he tripped and slammed into the muddy grass, rolling a few feet down a slight decline.

The guy who'd been circling her had changed his mind after Bailey had gotten head-locked. Now he and the sixth man, a muscular redhead, were converging on Roland.

The wizard held up his belt in a slow, almost lazy motion. Then suddenly, it flashed toward Redhead's eyes, hitting from what almost seemed to be an impossible angle. The man squawked and cringed, temporarily blinded, flailing uselessly with his arms.

Roland evaded him and turned to face the other man, a nondescript bearded guy who almost looked like a smaller version of Dan. The attacker charged, his shaggy head down, his fists forward.

There were only a few feet of dirt separating them, and that dirt looked perfectly flat. Yet, just before he was in range, the bearded man tripped over a small protrusion he hadn't seen.

"Shit!" Little Dan cursed, struggling not to fall, and instead stumbling against the side of the barn. By the time he got control of himself, Roland had aimed a roundhouse slugger straight at his jaw. It connected, rattling his skull and momentarily shorting out his brain's electrical system, and he slumped to the ground.

The amount of wind-up and force Roland had put into the punch, though, left him wide open, and one of Redhead's wild, grasping strikes took him behind the ear.

"Ow, fuck!" the wizard exclaimed, instinctively jumping forward a few steps before spinning to face his opponent.

By now, the man had mostly gotten his vision back, and he was prepared for a follow-up blow. But as he stepped forward, his foot sank into a hole in the ground that hadn't been there before.

"Whuh?" he drawled as he wobbled, his momentum ruined.

Roland was already on top of him, kneeing him in the

gut and hitting him in the side of the face with the flat of his forearm. He went down, yelping as his ankle twisted in the hole, and when he landed, he used one hand to cradle his foot and the other to cover his face in an unconscious gesture for mercy.

The wizard left him be for the moment and checked on Bailey.

The girl had returned to Gangly. He was about to spring back up at her, but she drove her foot hard into his ass, bruising the hell out of his gluteal muscles and knocking him back to the ground.

Dan Oberlin was back on his feet, however.

"That's it!" he roared. "It doesn't matter *what* you do, I'm gonna beat the shit out of you!" Foamy spittle flew from his lips.

Before Roland could intervene, Bailey tackled him again, clawing at his face. Her nails put red lines down his cheek as the back of his hand connected with her face, hitting her almost exactly where the good old boy in the bar had sucker-punched her earlier. They both ignored the blows, so deep were they in battle-fury.

Then Dan swung a powerful fist toward Bailey's fore-head, but she was quicker, ducking under it and smashing her fist into his groin. He pivoted, randomly punching and kicking as she ducked for cover. Then it hit him.

"Ohhhh, fffuuck," he groaned, his eyes bulging as the adrenaline melted away and the pain caught up with him. Clutching himself between the legs, he collapsed to his knees.

"There," Bailey panted, rubbing away the blood he'd

drawn from her cheek. "Just like I said. Now you *definitely* don't have the balls to mate with me."

With that, the scrap was over and done. Oberlin's henchmen were already stumbling away, not even looking at their adversaries. They made a beeline for the brown Chevy Blazer they'd come in, which was parked in front of the farmhouse.

Only Chins took the time to hook his arms under Dan's armpits, dragging his leader until the other man could properly stand—which might be awhile.

Soon, they were gone. Bailey and Roland watched them leave. For three or four minutes they both stood there, only a foot or so apart, leaning together on the old barn's wall and catching their breath. They'd won, and that was always a good feeling.

But they were both tired, and they'd both taken some good hits. They knew that kicking the South Cliffs' asses this time would not be the end.

"Shit," Bailey wheezed, "that was probably the best fight I've had in…I dunno, two months, at least."

"Wow!" Roland exclaimed, wiping the sweat from his brow and flicking it into the dirt. "Two whole months? I don't think I've ever been in a clusterfuck like that before. I've had a few fights, yeah, but that was a *brawl*. Goddamn."

Bailey looked at him over her shoulder. "Well, for supposedly not having much experience, you handled yourself well. Hell, I think I got it worse than you did, and I do this crap all the time. Who taught you to fight with a *belt* like that? That was some real kung-fu shit."

He smiled in his calm, subtly confident way as his lungs returned to normal functionality. "Oh, that was nothing, really. I might have used a few minor tricks to, uh, tip the scales in my favor. That reminds me, those guys are *really* clumsy. They need to watch where they're stepping and keep an eye on their balance. Everyone says footwork is one of the most important things in a fight."

Bailey shook her head slowly, wondering if what Roland had just said was an admission of using magic. She couldn't be sure. She'd been kind of busy with her own half of the fight, after all, but from what she'd seen, there were things that didn't quite add up.

And she was almost certain that a couple of the nearby patches of ground had been higher or lower or flatter than they were at the moment.

"Whatever," she said. "The important thing is, Dan ain't getting his precious piece of ass, at least not from me. But therein lies the problem."

Roland narrowed his eyes in concern. "You think he'll try again? With ten or fifteen guys instead of five? And possibly toting a couple of shotguns?"

"Maybe," she replied darkly, her voice lower and harder. "I don't think he'd go so far as to try to kill us or risk accidentally killing us trying to make me do the deed at gunpoint. My family is well-known and well-respected around here, and you can't get away with that level of serious shit in a little town like this. Everyone would know exactly what happened and who's responsible."

The wizard rubbed his chin as he considered her words. "I think you're right, but feuds like this don't end just because one side triumphs in a single fight. What do you think they *will* do?"

Bailey stood up and cast her eyes toward the wooded

horizon, looking southwest toward Greenhearth proper. "Whatever they can," she surmised. "They might just keep trying the same shit, ambushing us and trying to beat us up until I get tired of it and give in. *That'll* never happen, though."

Roland let out a sardonic chuckle. He was getting to know her quite well.

"Or," Bailey continued, "they'll try to make our lives a living hell through other means. Nobody with any sense likes the South Cliffs, but they've still got friends—alliances with other packs from nearby places in the mountains, things like that—and Oberlin Senior has money and connections."

"Right." The wizard rubbed his side where he'd been kicked. "And since there were no witnesses, they might be able to get away with slandering us and spreading rumors. I don't know if anyone would *believe* that six men, known to be asshole troublemakers, were the innocent victims of one girl and one guy, but you never know. Besides, the sheriff doesn't want me here, so it'll look bad if word gets out that I was involved in an…altercation."

Bailey clenched her teeth, and for a brief moment, she was almost as angry at the South Cliff pack now as she'd been just before the brawl had started. The whole community refused to leave her alone, and Dan Oberlin was the spearpoint of the whole damn thing: Operation Get Bailey Nordin to Open Her Legs.

Now Roland, who didn't have anything to do with it originally, might get in trouble, in addition to all the ways the Oberlins could make things even worse.

"Fuck," she growled. "I can't even call the sheriff or my

brothers, because then the shit would really hit the fan. The sheriff wouldn't believe we didn't start it somehow, and my brothers would kill Dan. We can't keep this up, Roland. We can't just sit around and wait for Dan and the other pricks to try whatever they have in mind next. Whether it's more brute force shit, or whether they decide to act like a bunch of high school girls and just spread gossip, it's going to screw us over one way or another, and sooner rather than later."

"I agree." His tone was dismal but not despairing. There was still energy and determination in him. She liked that. "Whatever they do, it will make a lot of noise, as well. And my three not-so-lovely ladies are still hovering around, so I'm almost positive they'll *hear* that noise and move in for the kill."

Neither of them spoke for a minute, and for the last few seconds, they turned and looked into each other's eyes.

Bailey broke the silence. "We need to get the hell out and fast," she concluded. "Out of this entire valley and away from anyone who knows me, just like you wanted to get away from anyone you knew in Seattle."

The wizard smirked in a darkly humorous way. "You're full of good ideas today, I have to admit. Any notion about where we should go?"

"Hell," she responded, suddenly feeling stupid, "I've never been outside this stretch of the mountains. You'd know better than I would where we oughta go. At least you've been between Seattle and here. That's a lot more of the world than I've seen."

Nodding, his eyes grew distant, and he thought for a few seconds. "Portland," he said finally. "Come on, let's go to your truck. I can direct you there. Just make sure your brothers take good care of my car in the meantime."

They both started walking, quick and purposeful, at the same time.

"My brothers," Bailey retorted, "taught me everything I know about vehicular maintenance. Well, Jacob did, mostly. And Gunney taught me some, too. Whatever. Point being, your car's in the best hands in Greenhearth. It'll be fine unless Dan Oberlin is even dumber than I thought and tries to blow up our pole barn with a big-ass jug of flaming moonshine or something. Good thing it's not in town anymore."

Roland snickered. "That would be something to see. Almost worth the loss of the car just for the novelty factor."

Bailey sighed. "Yeah, yeah. Not sure we'd agree about losing the barn."

They reached the Tundra, noting gratefully that the South Cliffs had been too eager for direct confrontation (and too eager to escape, a few minutes later) to bother sabotaging the truck. They leaped into their respective sides.

Bailey had the keys in the ignition almost before Roland could even pull down his seat belt. "Think we better hurry," she suggested. "The South Cliffs won't be back anytime today, but the cops are another story, not to mention your suitors. Word will get out fast."

Roland fastened his belt and glanced at her. "No long scenic route, then?"

"Nope," Bailey almost snapped. "Just gunning it out of Dodge as fast as, uh, reasonably possible."

Roland grinned. "That sounds pretty fast."

The girl shifted into drive, wheeled the truck around in a nearly complete circle, and shot mud out from under the tires as she barreled straight down the dirt road that would lead them back the way they'd originally come, through the forest.

She almost felt guilty, leaving the barn wide open with its doors wrecked, but under the circumstances, there wasn't much else they could do. They didn't have time.

As the truck bumped and rocked its way along the tortuous dirt road, Bailey reflected on their hasty decision and decided it was a pretty good one after all.

"Portland might be ideal," she opined. "It's the biggest city I know anything about. I hear things; we get a fair number of people from there passing through on their way to more interesting places, and some of them stop over for a bit. Also, it's far enough away to put some distance between us and the numerous assholes who seem to have collected in Greenhearth."

"Right," said Roland. "And it's not *too* far from home, for you anyway, in case we need to rush back. Obviously it will have more amenities than an abandoned farm—no offense intended—so we can lie low while things cool off with your wannabe boyfriend. Meanwhile, if we're lucky, we'll confuse my wannabe girlfriends. They'll probably expect me to keep heading east or south. Portland is doubling back, a classic evasive maneuver."

Bailey smiled, but then she squinted, thinking things over in more detail. "How big is Portland, anyway? I mean, it's smaller than Seattle, right? Yeah, I know, all this shit's on the Internet, but I never bothered to look it up. Didn't have a reason to."

Roland braced himself against the dashboard as they hit a nasty rut while going around a curve. "Portland's smaller than Seattle, but still pretty big. Large enough for us to get lost in. In a good way, I mean; like, to lose our pursuers. They'd have to look hard."

"Okay," Bailey acceded, "good. Could you, like, give me a frame of reference? Again, I've never driven around an actual city."

He nodded. "What I said earlier about the sprawl between Seattle and Tacoma and so forth pretty much applies to the Portland area too. As I understand it, that's every major city in America, really. Anyway, how many people are in Greenhearth?"

"Uh," she answered him, "depends on how you define 'Greenhearth' since the town proper has about seven hundred people, I think, but it goes up to around a thousand when you include all the rustics who live outside the town limits but are still, y'know, part of the community. The post office serves all of them, after all."

Roland nodded. "Right. Population of seven hundred, urban, and about a thousand in the metro area. If memory serves me correctly," he took a deep breath, "Portland has at least six hundred and fifty thousand people in the city proper, and when you figure in the greater metropolitan area, it rises to about, uh, two and a half million."

Bailey knew there were places where *millions* of people lived shoulder-to-shoulder with one another, but until now, such facts had been mere abstractions.

"So," he continued, "that would mean Greater Portland is approximately two thousand, five hundred times larger than Greater Greenhearth. Does that put it in perspective?"

Bailey stared straight ahead, silently, at the road as they came off the winding woods path and back onto the road that led downhill toward town.

She cleared her throat. "Well, shit."

The only other "customer" in the sheriff's office was some drunken derelict who'd wandered into town from one of the other, nearby communities. He slumped in a chair out front, barely conscious, the cops not even having bothered to restrain him while they processed his paperwork.

The woman ignored him, trying not to look at his shabby clothes or breathe the foul-smelling air near his body any more than she had to.

Meanwhile, the fat sheriff and his stupid-looking deputy were trying their best to ignore *her*, as well as her friends. Since they had not been helpful, that was fine with her.

She looked down into her hand, and her eyes suddenly bulged in surprise. Then she flipped her unnaturally red hair away from her face to see better. Her head snapped up, drawing the attention of the other two girls.

"Let's go," she said sharply. They hustled to her side and the three strode out the front door, not bothering to speak to the cops.

Sheriff Browne turned his head and watched them go. "You ladies get back to Seattle nice and safe now," he called after them.

None of the three paid his comment the slightest heed.

Once they'd gotten off the dirt road that led to the farm and brushed the edge of civilization again, Bailey and Roland changed their plans. Rather than drive through the middle of town, they took a minor detour through the residential side streets around Greenhearth's northwest corner.

Roland repositioned himself in the seat. "At least it's a smoother ride now," he commented. "And it's not like the town is big enough that going around its perimeter is a major delay. Hell, even I can tell we're almost to the highway, and I've never been here before."

"Yeah, yeah," Bailey riposted. "Stuff it. You and your 'metropolitan areas' that take two hours to drive across. If we were going the other direction, we'd probably make it to Idaho in the same amount of time."

They were now on a road that led straight south at the very edge of town, a cliff topped with pine trees to their right and a slope leading into Bailey's neighborhood to their left. There were only a couple of houses on the street, and in another quarter mile or so, they'd intersect the highway.

Greenhearth would be safely behind them in minutes.

"Hmm," Roland quipped, "not sure about that. The part of Oregon where nobody lives looks pretty big to me, on a map at least. I guess it depends on how many awful mountain roads we'd have to— *Oh, crap!*"

Bailey instantly saw what had interrupted him—a car had pulled out in front of them across the road, seemingly from nowhere off to the left, and she slammed on the brakes while spinning the wheel to the right.

"What the hell? Fucking drunks!" she cursed as the truck bumbled into the gravel and mud of the shoulder, just under the cliff.

The vehicle that had cut them off stayed where it was—parked perpendicularly across the road, almost completely blocking it. In the brief excitement, Bailey hadn't registered the make, but now she could see that it was a silver Jaguar.

Roland wiped a hand over his face. "Let me handle this," he murmured. With the air of an arachnophobic dad preparing to kill a spider for his daughter, he unbuckled himself and stepped out.

"Like hell," Bailey muttered and got out as well.

CHAPTER EIGHT

Three women piled out of the car and formed a rank in front of it. The afternoon's light was waning and half the clouds had returned, but Bailey could make them out clearly nonetheless—in part because they stood out like a sore thumb against a bleached white background.

The one in the middle, whom Bailey immediately pegged as the leader, was about the same height she was, thin bordering on downright skinny, and slightly orangish-looking, with hair that draped over most of the right side of her face dyed a strange purplish-red color. She had her hands on her hips, and long nails the same hue as her hair stood out against her short silver dress.

To her right was a darker-complected woman with black hair in a high ponytail. She was about an inch taller, with large breasts and full lips. She wore a tight black top and knee-length black skirt with heels and had a tiny black crossbody handbag.

To the left was a shorter, curvy blonde with a pixie cut and heavy blue eyeshadow. She was wearing a white sports bra under a sapphire-colored windbreaker jacket, along with equally blue yoga pants and blindingly white sneakers.

Bailey guessed the blonde was about twenty-three and the other two more like twenty-seven or -eight, although it was difficult to be certain since they were all wearing a ton of makeup. And perfume. They looked like high-roller party girls on their way to a nightclub, about as congruous with the people of Greenhearth as an elephant in Alaska.

"So," Bailey whispered, "Blonde, Brunette, and Fuchsia —a classic lineup."

Roland cleared his throat. "Excuse me," he said in a monotone, "you girls almost look familiar, I think, but you're blocking the road."

Fuchsia flipped her hair away from her face. "Shut up, Roland," she snapped. "What the hell do you think you're doing, running away like this? We *miss* you. Don't you know that you're *needed* back home?"

Somehow, she'd calibrated her voice in such a way that the inquiry came across as both deeply sincere pleading and a mocking sneer at the same time. Bailey's skin crawled at the layers upon layers of complex dishonesty it implied.

The brunette spoke next. "You didn't even leave us a message," she cooed. Her voice had a slight foreign accent, maybe Indian or Middle Eastern. Her fingers curled around the edges of her handbag.

"Yeah," the blonde added, loud and direct, "and who the fuck is *that?*" She gestured flippantly at Bailey without looking at her. "And why are you out here where cows aren't even in burger form and you can smell their goddamn shit in the air?"

Roland blinked. "Wait, how many questions is that? I'll need a minute to count them before I try to answer."

Fuchsia stared at him. "Gawd, you're so *cute*," she replied, her voice low and insinuating. "And this town has so much...*character*. All that's missing to complete the quaint little picture is some inbred-looking guy playing a fiddle and drinking moonshine."

They'd barely paid attention to her, but now Bailey was pissed.

"That's the South, you morons," she shouted. "And cows are mostly a Midwestern thing. If you smell shit, it's because it's leaking out of your ears. This is the *West*. Of course, we do have moonshine, but you posers couldn't handle a swig of it without ending up in the emergency room. And if there *were* a fiddle around, I'd shove it so far up your cooch that you couldn't even scratch your itch with the bow."

Not only the three girls but also Roland stared at her, bug-eyed and open-mouthed.

Fuchsia took a step forward and the other two followed her, the trio forming a sort of arrowhead pointing at Bailey.

"And, uh," the leader commented, the softness of her voice emphasizing her dismissiveness, "who are you, again? If you're going to talk to us like that, it seems like I should have, you know, *heard* of you."

Roland seemed about to stand up for her and tell them off, but Bailey had made up her mind to handle this herself, regardless of what he'd said.

"I'm his girlfriend, you whores," she stated.

The expressions changed on the three cosmetic-laden faces, and a tense silence blanketed the street. Bailey suddenly recalled a certain nasty old saying, something about a woman scorned.

Fuchsia, unsurprisingly, was the first to respond, although Bailey had to admit she was surprised by just *how* she chose to react.

"Oh, that is *bullshit!*" the woman shrieked.

Her voice bore no resemblance to the sultry, multi-layered oratory she'd used a moment ago. She extended a hand, her index finger with its reddish-purple nail sticking out like a bloody knife, pointing alternately at Roland and Bailey.

"He can't *get* a girlfriend! He's not some fucking alpha player, he's just a geek with a pretty face, a couple of savant talents, and really good genes. We have *business* with him, and it's none of your fucking affair. You wouldn't even know what to *do* with him, you stupid little hick slut!"

Bailey recoiled, partly a reflex at the woman's sudden deafening volume, but mostly out of shock at her stupidity. "'Little?'" she marveled. "You're the same height as me and look like you weigh twenty pounds less. Is anorexia the new fad diet where you're from?"

The blonde took a step forward. "Shut the fuck up," she snarled. "You're not even, like, relevant to this discussion."

The dark-complected one meanwhile glanced between Bailey and the wizard. "I think we should let Roland decide, like a beauty contest. It would not be much of a contest, don't you think?"

"Shit," Roland interjected. "I don't know. I mean, Bailey looks pretty good even *without* makeup. Or glamour spells."

Fuchsia's index finger went from horizontal to vertical, now indicating that he was not permitted to speak. "Be quiet, Roland. We'll deal with you after we dispose of this little unwashed peasant woman who thinks she's your girlfriend. She clearly has *no fucking idea* who she's shooting her mouth off to."

Bailey realized that things were about to get ugly. The polite young lady in the silver dress had used the phrase 'dispose of,' and the already tense mood was becoming downright dark. She admitted to herself that since she knew very little about magic, she had no idea what these witches were capable of.

Roland started arguing with the trio, urging them to grow up and leave him alone and so forth, but they continued to scoff at him and lob insults while slowly advancing a half-step at a time.

Roland's hands had descended toward his belt, as he'd done just before whipping the shit out of Oberlin's cronies, and without even realizing it, Bailey had shifted her feet into a defensive posture.

She and the wizard had just gotten out of one fight. They didn't need to stumble right into another, especially not with the sheriff already suspicious of Roland as a potential lightning rod for trouble.

Then Bailey had an idea, something that could turn the whole situation on its head. She pulled her cell phone out of her pocket.

"I'm gonna call the sheriff," she threatened, "unless you leave, right now. You're blocking traffic. Doesn't matter how *much* traffic a road gets, that's still a crime. You're also harassing us, and your behavior toward Roland here meets the official definition of stalking. Illegal and illegal. That's a minimum of three things the sheriff can book you for, and he happens to be a personal friend of my family's."

The witches didn't budge, but they didn't move any closer, either; they just stood and fumed at her. She could *feel* their hatred, almost like the heat of the sun.

She continued, "At the very least, you'll be detained. Put in the county jail while they decide what to do with you." She paused. "*That'll* earn you all an ass-kicking. Looking the way you do, in a country jail full of tough redneck chicks? Your pretty faces will get ruined, because, uh, witches get stitches for being little bitches."

She'd made that last part up on the spot, but it seemed to fit.

Fuchsia crossed her arms over her narrow chest. "Oh, ha-ha," she jeered. "Such wit. Rhyming, even." Despite her sarcasm, though, Bailey's words had gotten to her. It had finally occurred to the woman that she and her friends were not above the law, at least not here.

The witches exchanged glances, and Fuchsia went on, "Of course, you'd need time to make a call like that. And dear, I don't think you *have* that kind of time."

Bailey tried not to let the dismay show on her face. The trio was going to try something after all.

Roland jumped in front of Bailey, yanking his belt from his waistband.

"Hey, check it out!" he exclaimed with mock enthusiasm. "I'm *taking my belt off!* Makes it that much easier for you to get my pants off. All you have to do is get past the belt."

The witches bristled at the dual implications of what he'd just said, and while they were distracted, Bailey went ahead and made good on her threat. She speed-dialed the sheriff's office.

Browne answered.

"Sheriff?" she said quickly. "I found Roland. You'd best come pick him up right away. We're on North Ridge just off the highway. Oh, and there's three city girls blocking traffic with their car and acting like they're high on party drugs or something. Might have to deal with them, too."

"Goddammit!" the blonde swore, overhearing the phone call.

As soon as Browne promised to be there directly, Bailey hung up and returned her phone to her pocket. When she looked up, the witches had retreated three or four steps toward the safety of their Jaguar.

Fuchsia glared at her quarry. "We'll be back," she promised. "Roland, you know we can track your ass *anywhere*. If your ass goes to Elko, Nevada, we'll be there. If it goes to Charleston, South Carolina and boards a ship bound for South Africa, we'll be there, too. And then, before you know it, we'll have your ass in our hands."

She turned her eyes to Bailey, letting the idea sink in that Roland's ass would never belong to *her*.

The three began climbing back into their car. The tall, black-skirted brunette finger-waved at the wizard. "Bye, Roland," she said as though wishing him well after a pleasant dinner date.

"Yeah," the blonde added much more obnoxiously. *"Bye."*

Then the silver doors closed around them, and the vehicle's lights flashed on before it wheeled around away from them and vanished onto the highway.

Bailey exhaled. "Okay, now we need to leave double-time before the sheriff really does pick you up."

Roland didn't argue and both of them piled back into the truck, the Were starting it almost before the doors were shut. Bailey was pretty sure the witches had turned left, back toward Greenhearth, so unless they planned to double back, she ought to be safe to turn right toward Portland.

Traffic was a little thicker than usual since it was now "rush hour" and the highway had collected a few extra people going back and forth between civilization and the mountains. Still, it didn't take long for Bailey to make her turn, and soon they were accelerating to fifty-five, and then sixty miles per hour, the lights of the town falling away behind them.

"We made it," Bailey quipped, mostly to herself. "I half-expected to—"

Red and blue lights flashed in her rearview mirror.

Roland let out a sigh that quickly became a groan. "Well, we tried."

For a moment, Bailey almost contemplated stomping on the gas. She was so frustrated that stomping on *something* would have made her feel better. Rational thought returned in time to stop her, however. She slowly pulled the truck off to the side of the road and came to a stop.

Behind her, the police car looked familiar. Out of it stepped none other than Sheriff Browne.

"Well," she murmured, "at least it wasn't some random state trooper I don't even know."

She rolled down the driver's side window as the big man approached. "Hi, Sheriff," she greeted him.

"Evening, Bailey," he returned. "I didn't see any car blocking North Ridge. I do see Mr. Roland there next to you, though. So glad you were able to collect him."

Roland nodded vaguely in the man's direction without making eye contact, and all at once, Bailey felt like she'd somehow betrayed him. She shouldn't have made the phone call. They should have just taken their chances fighting the witches off and then made their escape as quietly as they could.

"Oh," was all she said to the sheriff.

He waved a hand at her in a beckoning motion. "Could I get both of you to step out of the vehicle? Slowly. Keep your hands where I can see 'em."

Bailey narrowed her eyes. "I wasn't aware we did any—"

"*Step out of the truck,*" he repeated, louder and harsher.

Sighing, Bailey did as she was ordered, wondering what the hell was going on. Roland shrugged and did likewise. If he was afraid of being hauled to jail, he was doing a pretty good job of hiding it so far.

Both stood in front of the driver's side door of the truck, hands clearly visible, although the sheriff made no move to frisk or handcuff them—at least so far.

He gazed at them steadily, glancing briefly at Bailey's ripped shirt and bruised face. "You're not under arrest just yet," he reported. "But you're not going anywhere until I ask a few more questions."

"Okay," Bailey replied. "What do you want to know, sir?"

His mustache bristled. "What I want to know is, what the hell is going on? Not only did I have those three lovely ladies camping out in my station all day—I was on the verge of making up something to arrest them for myself—but now I got five Weres trying to press charges for assault and battery. And you've clearly been in a fight."

Roland made a sputtering, snorting sound. The sheriff fired a sharp glare at him. Both he and Bailey knew he shouldn't have done that, but apparently he couldn't help himself.

"Sheriff," Bailey stated, "you know full well that's a steaming pile of utter horseshit." Disgust roiled deep within her. Oberlin and his gang had tattled on them after starting the fight themselves.

Browne nodded, but not in a way that suggested he agreed with her.

"Dan Oberlin came into my office along with five of his boys. You know the ones, I'm sure. They were all beat to hell, and one guy's ankle was twisted bad enough he might have to go to the hospital. According to them," he inhaled slowly, "they were dropping by to say hello, when all of a sudden..."

The sheriff spread his arms as if in surprise, but his face remained expressionless.

"Roland here leaps out of nowhere and attacks them. They say he turned into the goddamn love child of Bruce Lee and Chuck Norris, whipping 'em with his goddamn belt and beating their faces in, it being such a sneak attack that they didn't have time to react."

Roland neither confirmed nor denied this fascinating story, but it looked to Bailey like he was chewing on his tongue to keep from adding his two cents to her "horseshit" assessment.

"And," Browne went on, "Dan tells me that you, Miss Nordin, threatened to castrate him with your teeth. Now, what do you have to say to that?"

She huffed. "That's even more of a despicable lie if such a thing is possible. Five men who regularly cause problems around town went out of their way to follow me to my family's farm and break in, and they're saying that *we* attacked *them?* Come on, Sheriff. Just take a look at the barn door and you'll see the truth. I never said anything like that, either. Like I'd want his balls in my mouth! I can't read Braille with my tongue, for God's sake."

The sheriff's composure cracked and he turned his head aside, barking out laughter, but he quickly regained control of himself. While he wasn't looking, Roland reached out and patted her on the shoulder, and she smiled.

Browne turned back to her, his face stern once more. "Their story doesn't add up, I'll grant you that," he observed, "but right now, I need you to cut the shit and tell me what's really going on. Technically, any violence beyond the bare minimum needed to get away can be charged under assault and battery. You *should* have just shoved them aside, run away, and called us immediately, not hung around kicking the crap out of each other. That is, in fact, illegal."

She frowned. The man usually was lenient with low- or

mid-level fights like that, so his patience must have worn thin. Maybe she should have called him after all, but not her brothers, for sure.

"So," he continued, "why've I been so busy today? And what does it have to do with this guy?" He pointed at Roland.

Bailey locked eyes with the Seattleite for a brief second. Then, sighing, she looked at the sheriff.

"Sir," she began, her voice low and serious, "you know well that there are things in the world beyond what the news talks about. Such as *me*, for example."

He nodded. "Yes, I do."

"Well," she explained, "those three casino escorts or whatever the hell they are? They're more of those types of things. Witches, in fact. Real ones. They're after him for more or less the same reason that idiot Dan Oberlin and lots of other guys are always after me, and both of us are getting pretty tired of being treated like pieces of meat that need to shut up and get along to the butcher shop."

The big man crossed his meaty arms and continued to glower at the pair. "*Witches* coming all the way from Seattle, just for a hot date? I'll be damned," he murmured, and something about him seemed distant and strangely old, even as cars zipped by behind him on the highway.

Roland piped up. "So, sir, I take it you're, uh, aware of all the lycanthropy around here and such?"

"Shut up, boy," he snapped. "I'm aware of what goes on in my community, or at least I was until you showed up and made a mess of things. I will say," he looked at both of them, "that the last thing I want is a goddamn sorceress, let alone three of them, from out of state prowling around here and doing God knows what. But I'm still a sworn servant of the law, and you can't expect me to bend too far."

Bailey nodded. "We understand, sir. We were gonna skip town for a little while to let things cool off." She decided to leave out the details of where they were going, just as she hadn't bothered to mention that Roland was a wizard. Browne didn't need to know that.

"All right," the sheriff said softly, glancing again at her ripped shirt and the bruise on her cheek. "I'm gonna let you go. Technically I *shouldn't,* but arresting Pretty Boy here means he sits in the town jail, and as long as he's here, *they'll* be here. I doubt you'd disagree."

Roland almost shuddered. "Not at all, Sheriff."

The man waved a hand. "Go along, say, off to Portland, and stay there for at least a couple days. It's not too far, and it's big enough for you to lose anyone who might be looking for you."

Bailey bit her cheek to keep from snickering. The sheriff had advised them to do exactly what they were already planning.

"And," Browne went on, "I'll wrangle those witches for a little while longer. They probably headed back to the station in the hopes that I'd bring Roland right back to them. I'll pin them down for an hour with bullshit questions about their credentials and whether it was their car spotted blocking traffic, that kind of shit. At the end, I'll let slip that I saw you two heading southwest. That I figured you were making for Bend, maybe even Boise or Reno."

The girl closed her eyes briefly in relief. "Sir, that would be truly helpful. Thank you."

"Agreed," said Roland.

Brown uncrossed his arms. "Thank me later by *not* pulling crap like this again after you get back. And hold on a minute. There's one more thing. "

Bailey wondered what that could be. Knowing the man as she did, it would probably be an admonition not to get into trouble in the big city and to call her family when she arrived.

He surprised her by warning her about something else entirely.

"Be careful," he began, his voice only a touch above a whisper. "Unless you're bullshitting me, and I don't think you are, there's *witchcraft* afoot." He flicked his eyes to the wizard, then back to the werewolf. "Magic is still taken seriously here. People remember the old tales and the rules and punishments from the days when witches, and especially WereWitches, got burned at the stake. Some things don't change much."

Bailey kept her face impassive but nodded solemnly. "Yes, sir," was all she said, despite the sudden eerie coldness she felt. "We'll be careful."

"Aye," Roland agreed. "Thanks again, Sheriff."

Sheriff Browne turned and gave them a lazy wave over his broad shoulder. "Oh, and I suggest a change of clothes and some makeup. And call your family after you get into town." He trudged to his cruiser and disappeared into it.

Bailey motioned for Roland to return to the passenger seat. "Looks like we're free to go," she quipped. "Finally."

CHAPTER NINE

All the way to the outskirts of Portland, the couple in the black Tundra talked almost as comfortably as if they really were boyfriend and girlfriend.

Bailey laughed, trying to keep her eyes on the road. "What I can't figure out," she mused, "is how the hell we weren't able to smell them before the car shot out into the road. Goddamn, is there magic that can hide the scent of two gallons of perfume?"

Roland pinched the bridge of his nose and shook his head, chuckling gently. "I'll have to look into that. There are ways to manipulate such things, but, well, even magic can only do so much."

"Hah!" Bailey laughed. "So that's why they want your seed—to acquire your great and amazing power."

"You might be on to something there," he admitted.

They settled into a slightly more serious mood then.

"Anyhow," said Bailey, "I hope the sheriff was able to stall them, and that they're on the way to Bend by now. If we're lucky, they'll get lost somewhere in Nevada and be abducted by aliens."

"We can hope," Roland commented. "Although they would give a pretty bad impression of our species."

Bailey grimaced. "If I might ask, what are their names? I don't want to run into them again; I just feel like I should know who the hell they are."

"I can tell you that much," the wizard replied. "Just don't ask me for all the details of their backstories. I do not feel like going into it."

"Deal," said the girl.

Roland cleared his throat and closed his eyes for a second, waving his hand around the periphery of the truck. For a split second, Bailey felt something, then it was gone.

Her companion began to speak. "Just wanted to cloak us a bit. Sometimes people can hear their names when someone else says them aloud. Without further ado, the leader, the skinny one with the dyed burgundy hair, is named Shannon DiGrezza. She's the same age as I am—that would be twenty-eight, by the way—and has known me for the longest, but please don't ask me about that."

Bailey nodded. "Okay."

"The tall brunette with the little purse is Aida Nassirian. She's from a Persian-Armenian family from California, but they seem to have slid right in with the witch community in Seattle. I think she's a year or two younger."

"I see," Bailey commented.

"And," he finished, "the short blonde is Caldoria—or Callie—McCluskey, whom the other two collected recently, since she's only, uh, twenty-two or twenty-three, I think. I believe she's from Olympia and came to Seattle for the big city lights and so on. Nice to know she's not getting many of those in Greenhearth."

Bailey snickered again. "Small and boring towns have their advantages. Well, anyway, these witches—Shannon, Aida, and Callie—won't get the jump on us again. And if somehow they do, I'll just beat the crap out of them straight away before they can start talking out their asses and turn us into frogs or whatever."

Roland gave a spread-handed shrug. "That *might* work, simply because I doubt they'd expect it. But they might have shock-and-awe tactics of their own. Hard to say, and with three of them, even as, ahem, powerful as I am, I might not be able to counter them. They're pretty strong themselves. But I'm tired of talking about them or thinking about them."

"Fair enough," Bailey agreed. "Let's talk about Portland. We'll be there in, what, half an hour or so, won't we?"

"I think so." Roland sighed. "And we can talk about Portland in a few minutes. But first, you asked about the witches, so it's only fair for me to be able to ask about something involving you and your world."

Bailey's gut clenched at that, but she put on a cocky smirk. "Uh-oh," she said in an exaggerated tone. "Dunno if I like the sound of that."

The wizard put his feet up on the dashboard before he continued, "That weird, ominous stuff the sheriff said just before he let us go. What was the term he used? 'Were-Witches,' I think? I haven't heard of those before. And something about 'old tales' and burnings at the stake. What can you tell me about that?"

Frowning, Bailey wracked her brain for the best and

easiest way to explain it to an outsider. *Of course,* he'd ask about one of the things she was least eager to discuss.

"It's a nasty old custom," she began darkly, her voice low and monotone. "If a Were is found to have magical aptitude—you know, like yours—they're killed immediately. No werewolves anywhere will tolerate it; it's something all the packs agree on. WereWitches are abominations and must die."

Roland seemed legitimately surprised by this. "Well, that sucks. Have you seen it happen?"

"No," Bailey replied. "It's pretty rare, at least these days. Probably because my people have worked so hard to eliminate magic from the gene pool through that very tradition. I mean, it's not like it's a common thing everyone talks about, but the stories have kinda lurked in the background ever since I was a kid."

The wizard stared out the window. It was early evening now, the sunlight turning the hills and forests a darker green, while the sky took on an amber-orange tint.

"Old, ignorant customs," he remarked in a distant, almost philosophical way. "Every culture has its superstitions going back into prehistory that have persisted throughout the centuries. Did anyone ever mention *why* WereWitches are hated so much?"

"Not really," Bailey answered, "although reading between the lines, my best guess is that it would upset the social order too much. A werewolf with magic would be too powerful, and the pack Alphas couldn't boss them around. So, they're eliminating the potential future competition. Can't have Weres with extra gifts running around and taking over packs or starting their own. That would destroy the normal order of things."

Roland returned his feet to the floor of the truck, brushing away the mud he'd left on the dash with his hand and putting it into one of her ashtrays.

"Yeah, sounds about right," he agreed. "Most ancient traditions are either about keeping people from overthrowing the existing hierarchy or about stopping people from killing themselves. Like the dietary proscriptions in the Old Testament. They're mostly just ways for people to live in an environment where it's a hundred degrees every day in times before refrigeration and not die from eating spoiled food."

Bailey laughed. "Interesting. We don't, uh, read the Bible, actually. We have our own gods. Werewolves do, I mean. But I'll tell you about them some other time."

He perked up. "Please do. I enjoy learning about that kind of stuff. That reminds me of the third type of taboo— the ones on breeding. Those are all over the place too, aren't they? Like how in America, until fairly recently, it was frowned upon for people of different races to marry. Or how in India and Japan, people of different castes weren't supposed to get too friendly with one another, and so forth."

"Right," she confirmed. "People can't just, I dunno, let nature take its course."

He put his hand in his pocket, probably checking his phone, but he didn't take it out.

"Oh," he said suddenly. "By the way, you don't think you might have any magical aptitude, do you? I've noticed that you seem sensitive to things that are too subtle for most people to notice. Then again, I have no experience around Weres, so it could just be your heightened senses."

Bailey shook her head. "Nope. If anything, I'm pretty sure I'm less magical than most. I…well," she paused, sighed, and felt blood rushing to her face to grow cherries on her cheeks, "I didn't want to talk about this because it's really embarrassing, but…"

Roland looked at her, and his expression was warm and gentle. "It's okay. No judgment."

She nodded. "I can't change."

He blinked. "Oh. You mean…"

"I can't, you know, shift into a wolf-thing. I have the blood since both my parents are Weres, and I have the hearing and vision and strength and all that. I guess things go wrong sometimes, and I'm the proof of that. Even if I can't shift, I can produce Were children. That's been proven. There aren't so many females anymore that they can ignore me, even though as far as my people are concerned, I'm handicapped. "

She tried not to hang her head, but it shifted lower in relation to her shoulders, as though something was weighing it down.

"I see," Roland said. "Well, I hope I didn't embarrass you back at the house when I sort of asked for a demonstration, although I'm assuming your brothers could have handled it. Anyway, having seen you fight, you didn't seem particularly handicapped to me."

Her stomach fluttered again. She suddenly wanted to bat her eyelashes at him.

"Thanks. All things are relative, though. I guess you could say I had to learn to fight well in human form since I don't have Plan B to fall back on like most Weres do. A lot hardly ever change unless they're hunting deep in the woods, since, y'know, can't have normal humans seeing that. But to not be able to do it at *all* is strange."

For a moment, Roland wanted to put a hand on her arm, but she was driving, so he refrained. "Try not to worry about it. You got us out of town successfully, and being able to turn into a wolf wouldn't be very useful in Portland anyway."

By now, they were coming into the city's outskirts. Bailey hadn't seen anything too surprising so far, although traffic had gotten heavier. It did strike her as odd that the clusters of buildings didn't vanish after a few minutes and give way to wilderness. They just kept going on.

Still, out here, it was mostly just houses and gas stations and warehouses. No skyscrapers, not yet.

"In fact," Roland went on, "one of the strange things about cities, now that I think about it and have a little more experience with small towns, is that you kind of have to be on your guard all the time, but also very careful and restrained."

Bailey shot him a squinty glance. That didn't sound much different from what she was used to, but she was curious about what he meant.

"Like," he extrapolated, "there's *always* a really stupid, aggressive driver who's going to try to cut you off or tailgate you while you're on a crowded street during rush hour and all you want to do is get into the right turn lane. And there's *always* an aggressive panhandler who may or may not be a junkie, testing you to see how much money he can get off you. And there's *always* cops who wonder if you're a career criminal because unlike in places like Greenhearth, they have no idea who you are. They can't keep track of everyone personally here."

He leaned back in his seat and rubbed his eyes.

"You *always* have to be at least slightly on edge because of stuff like that, and you can *never* just cut loose and beat the hell out of these people because those same cops *will* arrest you and throw the book at you. You'll end up locked in a cell with people much worse than you are, or someone will just shoot you on the spot. There are so many different people everywhere that you're never quite sure who you're dealing with."

All of a sudden, Bailey felt her enthusiasm for their little venture waning. "That's…something," she stated.

She glanced at her fuel gauge. "Crap. I need to get gas, especially if the traffic in this damn place is going to be as bad as you say."

"Go for it," he said.

It was only another two minutes before a gas station hove into sight. Bailey pulled into the place on the right and wheeled the truck around to the proper side of an open pump. Once they came to a stop, she fished around in her pockets and found a twenty-dollar bill.

Roland glanced at her. "Do you need money for gas? You're chauffeuring me around, after all."

She shook her head. "I'll be fine for now. Maybe later, though, since I usually don't do this much driving. Thanks for the offer."

Opening the window, she waited for the attendant. Once he came, a pimply boy of about sixteen, she told him to put in $20 worth of regular.

As the fuel pumped into her tank, she noticed two guys with baseball caps and earrings hanging around near the air pump off to the side, looking at her and talking between themselves.

"Just stay right where you are," she growled under her breath.

The attendant let off the pump when the price display hit $19.87. She'd had about a quarter tank, and while this wouldn't fill the whole thing, it ought to be enough to last for a while. He replaced the nozzle and she paid him, then went inside to go to the bathroom.

When she emerged from the building, the two hat-bearers started walking toward her.

"Hey, there," one of them called, "looks like you're missing a piece of your shirt on the shoulder there."

She cursed silently, having forgotten about that, and wished again she'd thought to bring a change of clothes.

The guy went on, "So, like, if you want, I can take that off your hands and let you trade up for a complete one. Used to belong to my ex. Might be a little bit tighter on you than it was on her, though."

"What," Bailey blurted, pivoting to face them, "you gonna offer to pull out a tape and measure my bust while you're at it? Christ, neither of you numbnuts are drunk enough to be hitting on me. Go home and have another couple brews. Since you seem sober, you *oughta* have recognized that I'm the type who will shove your balls up your ass if you try anything with me."

The one who hadn't spoken yet laughed and said something like "Whoa-ho-ho! Feisty!" His buddy simultaneously whined, "Oh, man!"

The important thing, though, was that they stopped dead in their tracks and did not attempt to bother her further. She climbed back into the truck, started the engine, and got back on the road.

"Well," quipped Roland, "*that* was fascinating. You really are a magnet for trouble, aren't you?"

Bailey groaned and tried not to roll her eyes. "Not you, too. Everyone says that, and it isn't even me. I mean, did you see *me* go up to *them* and start talking shit? No. They started it, and I just provided them with the response they'd earned."

"True," Roland admitted, no longer attempting to hide his amusement.

Just after the gas station, they entered the southeastern suburbs of Portland. Traffic picked up almost immediately, and Bailey squirmed as she struggled to keep track of everything going on around her.

"Shit," she hissed under her breath as her boot stamped on the brake. A pickup truck had just pulled out in front of her, forcing her to slow down rather than risk having to wait another thirty seconds before he could turn onto the road.

Roland was nonchalant. "Don't worry, you saw him in time," he pointed out. "Also, stay in this lane. I think the road grows a right turn lane somewhere up ahead, but then it disappears again after a mile."

"Okay," Bailey replied. The day's light was fading to where half the motorists had their headlights on, and she wasn't used to seeing so much illumination at one time. "Damn, where do all these cars come from?"

"Oh, you know," Roland drawled, circling his hand around the cab. "Places."

She snorted. "That's helpful, thanks. Do you know of any places to eat around here? That steak sandwich back at the Elk was the only thing I've had today. And I'm already tired of driving, to be honest."

Roland shrugged. "There's always places. I'll keep an eye out. Just keep going for now, and we can head into the city after we find somewhere to eat out here in the suburbs."

Fortunately, he spotted a restaurant a minute or two later. "Turn here," he instructed.

It took Bailey a second to realize that she had to go down a side street and then enter a huge parking lot forming a kind of plaza filled with at least a dozen businesses. She spotted the restaurant, though, and headed toward it, parking a few hundred feet from the entrance.

"Well," she said, "looks like a family-owned place, at least. I figured it would be all chain restaurants here, or maybe weird vegan cafés or some shit."

Roland hitched up his jacket as he unbuckled his seat belt. "There are plenty of those, too. Something for everyone. This place looks nice and simple, not to mention popular."

It was around dinnertime and the place looked at least two-thirds full, so Bailey hoped they were staffed properly.

Once inside, they found the place to be agreeable—not as homey as the Elk, but nothing too strange by her standards, either. Just an all-purpose American diner. The waitress brought them water, took their order for coffee, and left them to peruse the menu, which was a good five pages long.

Eventually, Roland ordered a grilled chicken Caesar wrap with onion rings, and Bailey a pepper jack burger, medium rare, with fries. Then they both leaned back in their padded booth, sipping their coffee, feeling warm and good.

"At least," Bailey began, "we finally got some privacy and can relax a little. We don't have to base everything we do or talk about on, y'know, our mutual situations."

The wizard raised his cup. "I'll drink to that." He smiled, and she couldn't help mirroring it as they both took a long swig of coffee.

"Although," Roland added then, "we probably ought to talk about what we're going to do next. We'll have to find a motel or something. Wish I could say I had friends in town who could have us as guests, but I don't. Still, we might as well have fun while we're here."

Bailey pushed a lock of brown hair away from her face. "Yeah, I'll agree with all of the above, especially the part about having fun. Shit, I've been thinking about coming to Portland to do something like this for a long time. It just never seemed, I dunno, realistic."

For a second, his mouth twisted into a slight smirk and it looked like he was going to make fun of her, but then his eyes softened.

"Yeah, I know what you mean. Leaving home seems almost impossible until you actually *do* it. Then, suddenly, you can do anything."

Bailey worked her foot under the table and prodded Roland's ankle with her toes. "That sounds like a slogan for one of those inspirational posters, but I think you're right."

"Of course, I'm right," he gloated. Then his smile faded.

"Well, you can do anything *except* stuff that, well, stuff that certain of us can do but aren't *supposed to* in view of everyone else. You know what I mean, I'm sure."

"Right," she shot back. "Like the kind of stuff I *can't* do."

Blinking, he apologized. "Sorry. I suppose it would also apply to lifting a three-hundred-pound object with one hand. Not many girls can do that. In my case, of course, it means the flashier magicks."

She nodded. "Aye. You were using some back at the barn, weren't you? Against the South Cliffs? I mean, correct me if I'm wrong."

"I was," he confirmed. "Just minor stuff that isn't going to set off any alarms."

At that, he leaned back and stared at the ceiling for a moment. "You know," he muttered, "I understand the rules and why we have them, but it's hard not to be annoyed by all the constraints, not to mention the unpleasant prospect of having to deal with *them*. Just one of the harsh realities of life, I guess."

Bailey squinted. He was speaking as though he were referring to something obvious and well-known, but she had no goddamn idea what he was talking about.

"Them?" she asked. "Who? The witches? The other packs?"

He turned his eyes to her and gave her a blank look for a second or two. "Huh. You really don't know, do you?"

"I guess not," she grumbled, feeling foolish.

"Well," he went on, "no one is born knowing anything, so there's no shame in learning something later than someone else. *Them*, meaning the 'Men in Black.' That's not what they're actually called, but it's close enough. The people who keep a lid on supernatural things." His dour expression suggested he'd encountered them before and didn't recall them fondly.

Bailey suddenly felt the skin crawl between her shoulder blades. "Shit. I honestly never heard of them. I guess Greenhearth isn't important enough to be on their radar or whatever. There's seriously some agency or whatnot that goes around suppressing stuff? Stuff like, well, you and me, I mean?"

Slowly, the wizard nodded his head. "Suppressing information, mostly. It's not like they're out to exterminate us. At least, I don't think so, and if they are, they're doing a pretty bad job of it. But you can imagine how the rest of the world would react to the knowledge that witches and werewolves and lots of other things that go bump in the night are real."

Bailey thought about it. In Greenhearth, everyone knew some of the population was different from the rest, and there had always been a taboo, mostly unspoken, about revealing that information to outsiders.

Roland finished his coffee. "It would be bad to fire up the anxiety and paranoia and superstition of seven billion people. The results would probably make the Salem Witch Trials look like a Girl Scout marshmallow roast."

She glanced around, suddenly concerned that someone might be listening to their conversation. No one was sitting in the adjacent booths, though, and the nearest other patrons seemed absorbed in their own conversations. Even Bailey had trouble hearing them under the buzz and bustle of the place's ambient noise.

Returning her gaze to the wizard, she had to agree.

"Yeah, people can get finicky about things they don't understand. I mean, the folks in Greenhearth know me and my family, and even assholes like Oberlin. We're just part of the scenery; everyone knows the score."

Roland watched her in his calmly intense way, as though he were contemplating what it would be like to live in a small town with a big secret.

She continued, "We never talk about it with anyone from out of town. Hell, most people only know about werewolves from horror movies or old legends and stuff. They'd probably flip their shit if they knew that's what I am. 'Hide your cats, Bailey's on the prowl.'"

Roland bit down on a smirk at that.

She forged ahead. "Or, y'know, young mothers going all helicopter parent on their kids. 'Oh, no, Bailey's a WERE-WOLF! She'll eat little Billy the first chance she gets. My, what big teeth she has.' As if little Billy would even taste good. Probably all fat and sinew. You'd have to put him in the slow cooker and then season the hell out of him with a ton of pepper and steak sauce."

Mid-rant, her eyes had glazed over as her mind had turned absently to the problem of cooking low-quality meat. Then she remembered Roland and refocused on him, wondering for a second if she'd gone too far with that last joke.

The Seattleite was looking at her evenly although his mouth was doing strange things. When she focused again, he doubled over and cracked up.

"*Steak sauce,*" he cackled, wiping his eyes. "And the *slow cooker*. Classic. Holy shit!"

Bailey laughed as well. "I appreciate a man who's got a fucked-up sense of humor."

The words had just left her mouth when the waitress returned with their food, her mouth scrunching at Bailey's foul language in a family establishment.

"Hi," she said, choosing not to make an issue of Bailey's faux pas. "Here you go. You had the burger medium-rare, right?"

"Yup." Bailey made room for the heated plate and its pile of food. The server then slid the chicken wrap over to Roland. "Enjoy your meals. Let me know if I can get you anything else. Coffee refill?"

They both requested one, and the young woman promised she'd be right back with it. They dug wordlessly into their food, both hungry and comfortable with the other's silence. Besides, that way, the waitress returned with coffee before either had a chance to blab more about magic or Were stuff where she could hear it.

Bailey was about halfway through her burger when Roland spoke next.

"Honestly, though," he continued, picking up where he'd left off a few minutes ago, "the Men in Black are less of a problem than my people. Being the *kind* of wizard I am, all 'special' and shit, poses more difficulties than anything the outside world can come up with."

Bailey swallowed a large mouthful. "Yeah, I can see that. Your own people are the ones you have to deal with most of the time. I'm 'special' in my own way too, although in my case it's because of what I *can't* do."

She frowned and drank some more coffee. "And for that matter, what I *won't* do, such as marry someone like Dan Oberlin. Makes me wish I did have magic sometimes. It'd be a way to secure a better life, seems like, and you guys aren't pressured into arranged marriages."

Roland turned his eyes aside. "Well—"

"I mean, *you*," she cut him off, "you're a different case. But with most witches or wizards, it sounds like you've got actual *freedom*. Not gonna lie; I envy that."

Roland made a strange gesture, showing the palms of his hands, and her best guess was that he simply didn't know how to respond, and had therefore decided not to say whatever had popped into his head. That was probably for the best.

Soon they'd finished their food and coffee and gotten the check, which Roland insisted on paying. "It's no problem," he assured her.

It was dark when they headed back out to the truck, feeling much better after a good meal.

"So," Bailey wondered, climbing into the cab, "what's next?"

Roland had already opened the passenger's side door. "As long as you can handle driving in the city at night—which you should be able to do with me guiding you—I'm gonna suggest a night on the town."

They'd tacitly agreed that going to a nightclub might be a bad idea, even after getting Bailey a new blouse at a Walmart. Too much chance of it ending with her beating the crap out of people. So, instead, they'd headed toward downtown in search of entertainment that was quieter, simpler, and more cultured.

Bailey had no complaints.

Roland inhaled the cool, damp evening air. "I bet this place is even nicer now than it is during the day."

Walking beside him, Bailey deliberately bumped into him and pushed him gently away from her. She forgot just how strong she was, and he ended up stumbling a couple of steps toward the rail just to keep his balance.

"What?" he asked. "Do you have a personal attachment to Tom McCall and he died at night or something?"

"No," she said. "You dork. Get back here." She reached out with her foot, hooking it around the inside of his thigh, and drew him back to where he'd been. "Wouldn't want you to fall in," she clarified.

They were at Waterfront Park on the west side of the Willamette River, right next to downtown Portland. The trees and grass were fragrant, the air almost misty.

"Thanks." He straightened himself out and adjusted the seams of his jacket. "But yeah, in the morning, we should see some of the other stuff throughout the city that would benefit from the sun. The Japanese Garden, maybe, or that cathedral arch thing under the one bridge. I forget exactly where it is, but I'll look it up later. I'm a stranger here myself, after all."

They both were, and simply wandering around together through a place completely new and unfamiliar to them had a quality that was almost magical. Somehow it reminded her of the first time her father had taken her up into the mountains.

Passing a covered picnic area, they spotted a board

plastered with posters and advertisements. Roland had gotten a step or two ahead, and he slowed to glance at the sheaves of paper. Bailey did likewise.

Mostly it was notices for upcoming events in the park: music festivals, farmer's markets, stuff like that. One that was especially interesting to the girl since she'd never heard of anything like it back home was an ad for a new Vietnamese-Ethiopian fusion restaurant.

Next to that was a large poster that read MISSING PERSONS across the top in large bold letters. It displayed pictures of the faces of four girls and young women with their names listed below each.

"Huh," Bailey said under her breath. "Almost sound familiar."

Two of the missing girls had the same surnames as families in Greenhearth and other Were packs from different parts of the valley. She didn't recognize the girls, though, so it might have just been a coincidence. They weren't uncommon names.

Roland had wandered ahead, but, realizing Bailey was no longer beside him, he stopped, turned, and strolled back to her.

"What's that? Something wrong?" he asked.

"Eh, nothing," she told him. Part of her wanted to run out this instant, find those girls, and bring them to safety, but she knew that would be virtually impossible. Also, she didn't want to ruin the moment.

He rolled his neck around on his shoulders and stretched his arms. "Okay, then. Once we're done with this park, I think we should get some ice cream or something and, I don't know, maybe stumble our way into downtown and see City Hall. And the Sovereign, which is this apartment building with a cool mural on the side. I heard about it somewhere a while ago. This isn't the optimal hour, but still."

"Okay." She laughed, appreciating his quirky desire to do whatever he wanted, regardless of the time of day. "Promise me you'll protect me from anyone who jumps out of a dark alley wanting my ass, though."

He sighed. "I suppose I can make that promise, although you have a pretty good track record when it comes to protecting your own ass."

"That I do," she stated.

They walked the short distance to City Hall, which was nice enough, although Roland found it to be nothing special. Then he waffled about whether he wanted to bother with the Sovereign and its mural. He seemed to be getting tired.

Since the hour was getting late, Bailey thought they ought to start looking into renting a room. For a minute, the implications of that clouded her thoughts, but she shoved that crap aside. They just needed some rest was all.

Then Roland stopped dead in his tracks. He looked like he'd seen a ghost.

CHAPTER TEN

She almost swore aloud, but the wizard's bizarre behavior kept her quiet.

He'd begun slapping his right hip, then plunged his hand into his right jacket pocket, fishing around with fast grasping motions. His face was distant but intent.

"What?" Bailey quipped, hoping she didn't sound worried. "You got a party going on in your pocket there?"

For a brief instant, she had the crazy, stupid notion that he'd somehow read her mind with magic about the getting-a-room thing and had a typical male overreaction. But no, it couldn't be anything like that. He almost looked...scared.

She cleared her throat, being loud and obvious about it. "Seriously, what's happening?"

"Shit," he muttered. He sidled up to her, his hand now still since he seemed to have found whatever he was looking for. "Alarm, basically. Back when Shannon and her posse cut us off, while you were insulting them, I quietly cast a little charm."

Bailey arched her eyebrows. If it involved the witches, he was probably right to react as oddly as he had.

"A fifty-cent piece," he explained. "It's a big, heavy, obvious coin. I enchanted it to vibrate and jiggle around if they got close as an early-warning system, and a minute ago, it started going crazy."

His face fell, and he slipped his hand out of his pocket. "Now it's mostly still again. Just a slight tremor."

Bailey put her hands on her hips and looked in all directions, casting sharp glares at any cluster of people she could see. There were no suspicious trios of rich party girls anywhere in sight.

Sighing, she turned her eyes back to Roland. "They followed us, then. Obviously they didn't find us, but they must have seen through the sheriff's little story and come the same way we did after all. They might be in Portland right this minute."

He nodded sharply.

"Well," she continued, "is there any way they could be, y'know, tracking that thing? The coin. If it picks up their signal or whatever, couldn't they reverse it to find you?"

The wizard rubbed his chin and looked skyward. "It's possible," he admitted, "but in order to do that, they'd have had to get their hands on the coin, which I know they haven't. So, either they made a lucky guess and blundered into Portland on a hunch, or they're tracking me the same way they have been so far."

Bailey kicked the ground. They'd been having such a nice time, and now those three were ruining things again.

"We need to get out of here," she suggested. "And we're going to need someplace to sleep tonight anyway."

"Good idea," he agreed. They turned and strode quickly back to the nearby lot where Bailey's truck was parked.

Before she could offer further ideas, Roland came up with one of his own. "A low-end motel would be best. The cheaper and rattier the better, frankly. That alone ought to deter them. They wouldn't be caught dead at anything less than a mid-range national chain."

"Sounds about right," Bailey agreed.

They reached the truck and hopped in, buckling their seatbelts in tandem with Bailey's firing up the engine and pulling out of the space.

"Um," she asked Roland, "do you think traffic has died down by this hour? It doesn't look as bad as earlier."

He waved his hand. "Not sure. Probably somewhat. Large cities will always have some traffic, but rush hour is well over by now."

She turned her head so he wouldn't see her sigh in relief. "Okay, great. And, do you happen to know of a specific cheap motel, or do we just drive around randomly until we see one?"

"Drive," he said. "Pick a direction. North or west, since that will hopefully put us a bit farther from Shannon. In the meantime, I'll look on my phone and find one."

She agreed and piloted the truck out onto the street, heading north, parallel to the river.

As the wizard checked a map app for a suitable place, Bailey marveled at the width of the streets, the number of lanes, the number of cars, and the size, height, and density of the buildings around them. The architecture and the lights were beautiful in a way, but for someone used to farmhouses, small businesses, and the woods, it was all weird and intimidating.

Still, she'd enjoyed her time here so far, and she seemed to be adapting to the driving conditions. She knew how to handle her truck, so it was only a matter of figuring out the road system and watching for other vehicles.

"Okay," Roland said after a couple of minutes, "there's an economy place in North Portland that should be perfect. Low cost, mediocre reviews, underwhelming photos, and it's located in a working-class neighborhood near an industrial area. All of those factors should act as a pretty effective witch repellent."

"Good," Bailey agreed, although privately, she would rather have made an occasion of their stay here and chosen someplace nice.

The river started to bend northwest, and following Roland's instructions, she merged onto the freeway, then crossed the Fremont Bridge to the east side before turning left onto N. Interstate Avenue and continuing into North Portland.

Here the city became more residential, with traces of industrial elements. In general, it all looked slightly less rich. Roland told her to take a left, and they continued west through the metropolitan labyrinth.

"All right," he announced, "it should be coming up on the right. Just past this street."

The traffic light in front of them turned yellow and Bailey almost gunned it through, but she saw a police car in her rearview mirror and hit the brakes instead, jerking them both in their seats as the truck ground to a hard stop a few inches over the white line.

Roland inhaled. "Good call. Getting a ticket would leave a paper trail for people to follow. Not to mention the two of us might seem a tad suspicious, so they might search us and all that crap."

"Us?" Bailey mused. "Suspicious? Nahhh. Nothing strange about a hick werewolf and a runaway wizard heading to a flophouse for the evening."

He chuckled but said nothing until they were through the intersection. Then he instructed her to turn, which she did, and the cop car passed them without incident.

They pulled up near the office of the motel, which at least looked to be in good repair. Otherwise, it was about what they'd expected; it was the sort of place frequented by recent middle-class divorcees who were in the process of moving out and trying to cut costs, or city kids looking to party on the down-low. Bailey just hoped it wasn't also a hotspot for prostitutes and druggies.

Before Bailey could shut off the engine, Roland held up a hand. "Wait a minute, please. I need to do something."

She squinted at him but didn't ask questions, at least not yet.

He leaned back, took a deep breath, and closed his eyes. Then he held up both hands, each twisted into an odd configuration, and moved his right hand in a circle as if scattering dust or water around them. His lips moved, but no sound came out.

Bailey felt something—a strange tingle on her skin, almost as though a cold breeze had blown through the cab of the truck, although no such thing was obvious. It was more in her head than in the air.

Magic? Nah. Old trucks had odd cracks.

Roland opened his eyes and lowered his hands. "There," he stated. "That ought to obscure our presence and make us harder to pinpoint, even though those three would much prefer to hit up the local Marriott or something."

They both unbuckled and stepped out of the truck, Bailey stretching her arms and legs.

"I'll handle renting the room," Roland offered. "I have experience with that sort of thing. Wait with the truck, and keep an eye out for a goddamn silver Jaguar XKR."

She'd been about to protest since it seemed patronizing of him to act as though she couldn't handle something as simple as renting a room. Granted, she'd never done it before, but how hard could it be?

But once he finished his statement, she decided he was right. Someone should act as lookout, at least until they were safely checked in and could park the truck somewhere out of sight before getting themselves behind a nice locked door.

"Okay." She shrugged. "Just holler if you need me to rescue you."

He smirked and gave her a thumbs-up, then walked casually into the office.

The night was getting chilly, and Bailey climbed back into the vehicle after three or four minutes. It embarrassed her a little; she'd spent plenty of time outside, and only the coldest days of the winter usually bothered her. There must be something different about the quality of the atmosphere in the city —a particular chill associated with lots of wet concrete.

The door opened a moment later and Roland strolled out. He motioned for her to roll down the window.

She did, but immediately mouthed off to him. "What, you're physically incapable of getting back in the cab now?"

"Ha-ha," he said flatly. "No, I was just going to say that I'm physically capable of walking to our room, which is around that corner there." He pointed. "You bring the truck around, and I'll meet you there."

"Fair enough," she muttered.

He leaned closer and added in a low voice, "Try to park somewhere no one will be able to see the Tundra from the street."

"Yeah, yeah. Already thought of that, but it's good to know that you're as smart as I am." She smiled.

He widened his eyes in mock hurt and surprise. "You doubted me? Shock!" He turned and ambled down the walkway ringing the building.

Bailey followed him, pulling ahead of him once she attained the rear lot. She glanced around to get a feel for the line of sight from the road and parked close to the structure near the center of the back wall, then climbed out and locked up.

Their room was two doors to the right of where she'd left the truck. Roland was in the process of fumbling with the keycard. He may have had experience with this sort of thing, but he wasn't an expert yet.

"Y'know," she told him as she walked up, "I just realized that we forgot to bring toothbrushes. Or, uh, deodorant and all that." She sighed, feeling more like a country bumpkin than ever. "Crap."

The wizard finally succeeded in opening the door, and

he held it open for her with his foot while he slipped the card back into his pocket.

"Eh, well," he drawled, "it's an economy place anyway. Every motel provides soap, and they might have some courtesy mouthwash, if nothing else. If not, we'll buy some in the morning. And in the meantime, I promise not to comment that you still smell like you were fighting in a barn earlier today."

She planted a gentle punch in his stomach as she walked past. "That's the smell of victory, my friend, so watch your mouth."

"*Oof*," he grunted, his gut tightening under her fist. It might have been genuine. "I'll keep that in mind."

They flicked the lights on and looked around. The room was serviceable. No-frills, but it was reasonably clean and had what they needed.

Bailey piped up. "This'll do. To be perfectly honest, well, it woulda been nice to stay somewhere a little fancier. More fun. I've never done anything like that—had the royal treatment in the big city."

Roland caught her gaze, indicating that he was paying attention, but he grasped that she was about to say more, so he waited.

She went on, "And with your three, uh, suitresses—is that a real word?—hot on our tails again, I guess we're gonna have to keep our heads down and focus on staying ahead of them. That might make it hard to see the Japanese Garden and that arch thing you mentioned."

She allowed her head to hang a little.

Roland only said, "I'm sorry." Given his tone and his

face, he meant it, but not to the point that he was admitting any fault. And really, it *wasn't* his fault.

"I'm sorry too," Bailey continued, her words coming faster than she'd intended, "for complaining just now. That's, I dunno, out of character for me. I'm not a girly-girl. I'm used to roughing it and being self-sufficient, and it's not like I'm trying to guilt-trip you for not spending enough money on me or anything like *that*. It's just…"

Her eyes went distant as she searched for the right way to articulate her feelings.

"It's more like, well, I've enjoyed the time we've spent together on this little adventure since you rolled into town, and I was kinda hoping we could make a fun vacation out of this, y'know? But now, having to stay here and hide our wheels? Well, it's a blunt reminder that we're damn near fugitives. It's not a—" she swallowed, "an excursion."

She'd almost said romantic excursion, but had stopped herself at the last instant. The word "romantic" could mean a lot of different things, and the old definition had more to do with adventure than with couples. That was what she'd meant, of course. But she didn't want Roland to get the wrong idea.

His eyes were soft, and his face almost sad.

"I understand," he intoned and sat down on the slightly dingy loveseat before he continued.

"I've had fun too, and you've helped me a lot—really—so I'd rather have made this more pleasant for both of us. I like the thought of being your tour guide for the world outside Greenhearth, even though I'm kind of new to the world outside Seattle myself. But it is what it is. This is what my life has been lately—shitty motels, dive bars and restaurants, back roads, strange hours, and suspicious cops. It's the life you end up living when you're on the run."

Somehow, hearing him say that hit her right in the gut. She wanted to put her arms around him and tell him it would be okay, but she didn't. At least, not the physical part.

"It's okay. Or, well, it *will* be okay. We're gonna figure this out. I understand, though, and I won't complain again. We're in this together, and we have to do what we have to do, I guess."

He smiled gently. "Thank you, Bailey. I mean, we'll still be able to have *some* fun, I'm sure, but we have to watch our asses."

She clenched her teeth, a powerful fury rising up in her before she even knew where it had come from.

"Goddammit. Wish we could just eviscerate those three bitches and be done with it. At least with the South Cliffs, we were able to kick their asses and send them back to Oberlin's house with their tails between their legs."

He laughed at that, and she had to admit she liked the edge to the sound. He didn't seem like a vicious person by nature, but he'd clearly enjoyed beating the hell out of them. They'd deserved it, after all.

"True that," he agreed. "Shannon, Aida, and Caldoria are a little more complicated to deal with, though. First of all, it's harder to get away with beating the hell out of women, even if they pretty much have it coming, let alone *eviscerate* them. Good word, by the way."

"Thanks." She smirked.

"And," he continued, "there's the whole witchcraft element. But yeah, I'll confess to wishing some things were different, too. That there was a way to go back and make different choices at different times. Like, the idea that our whole lives might be different now if we'd just done one little thing instead of one other little thing years ago."

Bailey closed her eyes. "Yes, I know what you mean. I truly do."

For another hour or more, they stayed up and conversed, Bailey sitting on the bed while Roland stayed on the loveseat, exchanging their thoughts and feelings on their lives and all they'd done.

They talked about random incidents in their pasts, fleeting impressions that were lodged in memory, and minor cases of taking one road instead of another, and wondered about all the possibilities they'd missed by doing so. They imagined what it would be like to live in a world without the stresses and pressures they continually labored under and to prevail in a life where they were masters of their own fates. Somewhere in the middle, Roland cast a healing spell on them so they'd be functional in the morning.

Eventually, Bailey laid down on the bed, a warm and comfy grogginess coming over her. Her voice slowed, while Roland's grew distant. The rigors of a very long day caught up with her, and she passed out.

The wizard sat quietly where he was for five or ten minutes as the young woman slipped into a deep sleep. He watched her for a bit. It occurred to him that she might suddenly fly awake and chew him out for it, but he wasn't leering at her. She was attractive, yes, but mostly he was just thinking.

She was his companion now, his partner. Not in a

romantic sense, of course, their cover story of being in a relationship notwithstanding, but the two of them would have to see this through. They were now committed to each other's well-being.

Looking at her, he realized he could have done far, far worse. He was lucky.

He stood up and moved to the other side of the bed. Bailey was lying halfway across the damn thing, and knowing he risked awakening her, he put his hands under her arms and hauled her into a proper position, then put a pillow under her head so she wouldn't wake up with an aching neck. Then he took the covers and draped them over her. She stayed asleep.

Stretching and exhaling, he went into the bathroom to relieve himself, wash his hands and face, and rinse his mouth—just with water since sadly, the room didn't come with courtesy mouthwash after all.

"Should have bought it in Walmart when we got her the blouse," he whispered to himself in the mirror. "Oh, well. We can always buy some tomorrow."

He knew problems with money might be lurking on the horizon, but for now, he wasn't worried about it.

Once he was ready to sleep, he returned to the main room and hesitated for a moment halfway between the bed and the loveseat.

"Eh," he grumbled, then chose the loveseat.

Even if he was a virtual transient these days, he still came from a good family and liked to think of himself as a gentleman. Climbing into bed next to a woman he'd only known for a day without her permission seemed iffy.

And, he ruminated as he reclined and got comfortable,

he had no idea how a Were-female would react upon waking up and finding a stranger sleeping next to her.

"Knowing her fiery-ass temper," he murmured as the haze of pre-sleep came over him, "she might rip my torso open before she even knew what she was doing. I don't think either of us want that kind of misunderstanding."

Roland liked her; there was no use denying that. However, she was arguably a member of a different species, one he only knew about from books, legends, bull-shit gossip, and the last few hours' worth of experience. He preferred not to take unnecessary risks with things he did not yet understand.

He yawned and drifted off to sleep, dreaming of Seattle on its sunnier days in his distant childhood.

***

Bailey woke up having no idea how long she'd slept, and it took her a second to remember where the hell she was. As vision and hearing returned to her and she stretched her body under the heavy covers, she recalled.

The motel in Portland. With Roland.

Glancing around, she saw him snoozing on the loveseat across from her. She wouldn't have minded if he'd slept in the bed, as long as he hadn't tried anything stupid and or hogged the covers or snored too loud.

There was a clock on the nightstand: 8:47 in the a.m. She wasn't sure when she'd fallen asleep, but it couldn't have been any later than midnight, so she'd gotten enough rest. It had been a tiring day—two fights plus a road trip. That had to be some kind of record for her.

She slid off the bed and made straight for the bathroom, closing the door to use the toilet and then splash cold water on her face. Roland woke up since she heard him shuffling around, followed by the floorboards creaking as he stood.

He knocked on the door. "Hey," he asked, "who the hell is in my bathroom?"

She snorted into the sink. "Not yours now, boy. Wait your turn. I'll be done in a minute."

After she let him pee, they took turns taking a quick shower. Bailey had washed her hair yesterday morning, so she figured she could let it go for today. Somehow, she didn't feel like dealing with wet hair when they couldn't even brush their damn teeth.

"So," Roland said as they settled back into the main room, "I think we need to keep moving. We can probably spend the first half of the day in Portland—get breakfast, see and do something—but by afternoon, we ought to push onward toward…I don't know, somewhere else. It will depend on whether or not my fifty cent piece goes off again."

Rubbing her eyes and wanting a cup of coffee, Bailey agreed. Until they could find a way to get the wizard to more or less permanent safety, it wasn't smart to hunker down in one place.

She confessed, "I don't know how I'll be able to keep up running from place to place for too long. Sooner or later, I'll need to get back home." That reminded her, her brothers should be going crazy about now. She should have called.

A stormy cocktail of emotions struck her all at once.

Even though she'd only been gone for one night, she was homesick. She'd never been away like this. Never.

At the same time, she knew that what she'd just told Roland wasn't true. She could, in theory, just run away with him. Part of her wanted to say, "Fuck it" and do exactly that. Another part of her was ashamed for even entertaining the idea.

"First, though," Roland offered, "before we come to any major decisions, I propose food. My treat. I'm famished."

"Amen to that," quipped Bailey, smiling.

She warmed up the truck while he went into the office and checked them out of the room. Rather than pull up to the door, she waited for him to come around the rear again on the off-chance he might have seen—or felt—something suspicious up there.

He climbed into the passenger's side. "Well, no disturbing pocket vibration so far," he stated.

"*That's* always encouraging," Bailey remarked.

After filling the tank at the gas station next door, they found a restaurant specializing in breakfast and brunch about a block and a half east of the motel. It was doing a modest business, which hopefully meant a shorter wait time.

"Right now," Bailey said, "I'm pretty sure I could eat enough omelets for both of us. Meaning two. Three or more might be a bit much."

"Hmm," Roland pondered. "We could order three and split the third one."

They ended up doing just that, to the initial confusion and later amusement of their waitress, an older lady who seemingly enjoyed the opportunity to take down an unusual order.

The pair sipped their coffee.

"Roland," Bailey asked once they had some privacy, "I was wondering. Where do you get your money? Can you really afford all this? I mean, I kinda got the impression that your family's pretty well-off, and obviously you've been managing so far, but…I dunno. Just curious."

His mouth took a sour twist. "I was afraid you might ask that," he muttered.

Bailey was suddenly concerned and a bit irritated. That sounded like there was something he should have told her sooner, but she *was* curious.

"I *am* asking that," she pointed out. "Speak."

"Fiiiiiine." He sighed. He shot a quick look around to make sure no one was within earshot, then turned his face back to her.

"So," he began, "one of my greatest magical talents is *manipulating* things, kinda like what I did with my belt back at the farm. But it goes beyond telekinetic stuff like that. Some time ago, I figured out a little…shortcut for procuring funds."

Bailey wondered if he meant counterfeiting, but she'd seen him pay for things with cards, not cash. Then again, she supposed he could have counterfeited a lump sum, deposited it in a bank, and be drawing off it with his debit card.

"I'm all ears," she said.

He coughed and went on, "I run fake credit card applications. Just keep re-rolling new ones with new limits. The details are a little technical, but trust me, it works.

Even saved my life a few times, you might say. The down-side is that the goddamn things always fall through after a while, and then they're traceable."

Bailey's eyes widened. "I'm having breakfast with a criminal? Shit!" Roland didn't react, so she added, "Although like the cops back home said, getting into fights all the time is technically illegal, too."

Roland laughed. "True. Most people aren't as innocent as they seem."

Bailey's face fell. "If they're traceable, though, aren't you gonna end up with a bunch of debt collectors riding your ass pretty soon?"

He shrugged. "Meh. I'm keeping tabs on all of it. I'll pay them back soon. Well," he glanced around again, "I'm hoping to pay them back once I can settle down and secure a normal income again."

His eyes shot up. Following them, Bailey saw the server approaching with their food, so she shut her mouth for the time being on the subject of illegal activities.

The waitress balanced a large tray next to the table. "Ooookay there, young folks," she proclaimed. "Three omelets for ya. Nice and hot, so watch the plates. Can I get you anything else for now?"

Roland and Bailey helped her arrange the plates and asked for a coffee refill, but that was all.

"Sure thing!" the lady agreed.

They tore into their meals, and Roland continued his story between mouthfuls of fluffy egg, meat, veggies, and melted cheese.

"Thus far, the only reason the witches haven't caught me," he paused to chew and swallow, "is because I keep staying in places they wouldn't think to look. For being individuals with magical powers and expensive educations, they're not terribly imaginative people. Except when it comes to fashion, I suppose."

Bailey almost spat out a mouthful of food at that. Instead, she forced it to go in the opposite direction.

"Yeah, good observation," she got out.

"Plus," he added, "I've been staying in low-end places. They're too fastidious or not tech-savvy enough or whatever to catch onto the fake cards and identities. Yes, I was using a fake ID previously, but I ditched it before I came into Greenhearth—which was a good thing since your sheriff would probably have gone apeshit if he'd found it."

Bailey finished her coffee. "You're a clever man, Roland." She snickered. "Maybe a little too clever from the sound of it."

He waved a hand at her, and his smile was a tad arrogant. "I've heard it all before. Unfortunately, cleverness only goes so far against psychotic, obsessive persistence." He sighed. "I just wish that their—the witches'—parents or employers or friends would get on their asses and make them give it up. They must have someone who's willing to say 'Young ladies, you come back home this instant' in a stern voice. Right?"

"Who knows?" Bailey remarked.

Soon they'd finished their meal. Roland had a little trouble with the extra half-omelet, but Bailey was able to make up the difference, and they stacked the three plates on the end of the table. The waitress materialized a moment later to collect them.

"I'll take those and bring you your check. Together?"

"Yup," said Roland.

"Okay, then." She trudged off.

In the pleasant afterglow of a good meal, Bailey leaned back and then turned to look out the window. Her breath caught in her throat.

"What the ever-loving *fuck*?" she gasped.

Roland tensed immediately, his own eyes snapping reflexively to the glass. "What is it? It's not Shannon. I don't see her, and nothing from the coin. Is it—"

"It's not your lady friends," Bailey informed him. "But it's just as bad."

CHAPTER ELEVEN

Bailey couldn't believe it at first. Her brain tried to tell her it was just a paranoid hallucination, but no. She'd seen the damn thing for the three entire seconds it took to drive past the restaurant and vanish around the corner.

She steeled herself, gritting her teeth as she spoke to the Seattleite.

"It's Dan Oberlin's butt-ugly SUV." A subtle tremor of rage went through her. "Not that brown thing they had at the farm; that must have belonged to one of his boys. This fucker, I'd know anywhere."

Roland blinked and gave her a cockeyed look. "Are you sure? Somehow I didn't peg them as the types to venture out of town any more than you."

"Like I just said," Bailey grated, "I'd know it anywhere. God, what an awful piece of shit. 2008 Chevy Suburban, white, so it picks up new goddamn mud stains on a daily basis because Dan Oberlin is a fucking moron."

The more she thought about it, the more she was sure

she hated the vehicle almost as much as its owner. Maybe more.

"Everyone around town knows that shit-ass horrible piece of white-trash crap with its fucking stupid big black spinner rims and its gaudy chrome lips and its bitched-up lifter kit that he tries to use to lift it *beyond all reason* like a fucking dipshit. And worst of fucking all, that horrible blue and purple wraparound flame decal *fuckery* that Gunney degraded himself by fucking putting on."

She balled her hands into fists. The wizard remained silent.

"I told him," she ranted on. "I said, 'Gunney, do *not* accept that shitfaced bastard's goddamn money for a *blue and purple flame job* on a white SUV. Not a truck, a fucking *sports utility vehicle.*' But nooo, old Gunney told me that he's a paying customer and the customer's always right. I did *not* do that shit. The other guy, Kevin, did it. I fucking refused. What a goddamn fucking bitch-ass piece of sub-redneck shit."

Roland stared at her, mouth agape. The waitress also returned with their check and stood blinking politely as Bailey hastily wrapped up her profanity-laden tirade.

"Sorry," she said to the older lady. "I just saw *the* worst truck in Oregon, if not the world. Trucks are, uh, kind of important to me."

The woman nodded. "I guess so. Anyway, here's your check, no hurry on paying. Have a nice rest of the day!"

"You too." Roland smiled and waved as she hustled off.

Once they were safely alone again, the wizard turned back to his companion. "Did you see Dan Oberlin driving it?"

"No," Bailey admitted, "but who the hell else would drive something that looked like what I just described? For fuck's sake!"

"Good point." He shrugged. "Anyway, that's all the more reason to get the hell out of here. Sadly, we might have to skip the gardens. Why would Oberlin be in Portland, though? Is this normal for him?"

The girl shook her head. "Yeah, maybe some other time on the gardens. And I have no idea. He and his crew sometimes go to parties and shit in other towns in the mountains, but I've never heard of him coming into the city. Kinda coincidental. Makes me think they're after us for revenge."

The dark implications of that sank in as silence reigned.

Roland was the first to break it. "I suggest, then, that we don't bother them or otherwise get their attention."

"Yeah," Bailey acceded. "Much as I'd love to kick their asses just for driving that…*thing*, not to mention everything else, we don't need the extra trouble right now."

They used the bathroom quickly and then beat feet out to the truck. To both their surprise, just before she climbed in, Bailey's phone started ringing.

"The hell?" she grumbled, pulling the device out and checking the number. "Well, I'll be damned."

She answered, "Hi, Gunney. What's up? I was planning to call. Sorry about that."

"Bailey," the old man said. "Jesus, are you okay? Your brothers told me the gist of it, but we've all been waiting to hear from you. Didn't the sheriff tell you to check in when you got to Portland?"

Her shoulders slumped. He was right; she should have

called. But focusing on her adventure with Roland, not to mention the flight from the witches, had been kind of distracting.

"Yeah, I forgot with everything going on. I apologize. Don't get your panties in a wad. I'm fine. Also, sorry I won't be able to make it back in time for my shift today, but you can give it to the new girl. Like I said, she needs the hours."

He made that rough-edged sighing, grunting sound he always made when he was impatient to deal with something important. "Listen, I'm not worried about that for now; we'll be okay. Did you hear the news? You didn't have anything to do with that, did you? Shit, everyone here's talking about it."

Now she was confused, and Roland, watching her and listening in, frowned in concern.

"What news? Calm down, old man, and talk sense. I've been busy trying to figure out the goddamn roads in this place. Don't have time to—"

He cut her off. "The missing girls. From Greenhearth. Remember yesterday when I told you about that girl from the south side who went missing? I was gonna send a card to her parents. Well, there's another one gone now—Lauren Heuerman. We just found out."

"Holy shit," Bailey blurted. Suddenly, the poster she'd seen in the park last night flashed in her memory.

"And," Gunney went on, "guess fuckin' what? The South Cliffs all happened to leave town at about the same time. The initial assumption was that they went to go get drunk with their dipshit friends on the other end of the valley after your fight, but once we all heard about the girl…"

Something in Bailey's spine went cold at that.

"Gunney," she replied in a low voice, "you don't think…"

"I do think," he shot back, "that they might be involved. That's everyone's suspicion. I mean, innocent until proven guilty, but let's just say the police are on the same page as everyone else. Bailey, this is important, so I need you to tell me. Do you know anything about this? Did you have anything to *do* with it?"

She knew he was concerned about her, but the question stung anyway.

"*Hell,* no," she almost shouted. "I came up here to get *away* from Oberlin and to help Roland here evade his stalkers. And before you ask, I'm sure he didn't have anything to do with it either."

There was a lengthy pause on the other end of the line. "Okay, fine," Gunney responded.

"However," Bailey added, "I'm almost positive I just saw Dan's POS drive by five minutes ago. I assumed they were looking for me. Since when do they get to Portland?"

The old man exhaled noisily. "Fuck," he muttered. "Girl, you take care of yourself, you hear? Be careful, watch your back, and come home as soon as you reasonably can. I'll tell everyone you're okay for now, but this isn't a good time for anyone."

"Okay, Gunney," she said. "Thanks for letting me know what's going on. And have faith in the new girl. She'll do fine."

"I will. Bye." He hung up.

Suddenly feeling like she could use a beer, Bailey slipped the phone back into her jeans.

Roland caught her eyes. "I overheard most of that."

She folded her arms over her chest. "Yeah, I'm sure you did. He was practically hyperventilating. He's a cool old guy, but every once in a while, he flips out when something's, you know, serious."

"Well, it *sounded* serious," Roland insisted.

The werewolf ignored him for the moment. She was thinking.

Lauren Heuerman was a Were. Gunney hadn't named the other girl, the one from the south side, but Bailey would not have been surprised if it turned out that *she* was a Were, too.

And those names on the poster last night had been familiar, which meant they could also be Weres. What the fuck?

Roland coughed in a loud, theatrical way. "So, I'm thinking we should do something, such as step into the vehicle," he suggested, "and then figure out where we're going next."

Bailey nodded sharply. "Into the vehicle, yes. But I know exactly where we're going—after Dan Oberlin's shitmobile."

Again, the wizard's mouth hung open for a second. "Uh, Bailey? I *really* don't think that's a good idea. We're trying to keep a low profile here, and you agreed with me five minutes ago that dicking around with those idiots would be an excellent way to fail at that."

"Yeah, well," she said sharply, "a lot has happened since then. Get in. We're going hunting."

They opened the truck and hoisted themselves into the

seats. Roland waited until he was buckled in before he tried arguing with her again.

"You know," he began, "instead of trying to chase them down or whatever it is you have in mind here, you could just call Gunney back, tell him our current location, and have him inform the police that their vehicle was sighted here. That way, they could start sweeping the area, and we wouldn't have to deal with Oberlin *or* the cops."

She snapped her head toward him. "Stuff it, city boy. First off, we can't call the police. This is a pack matter. *The pack stays together*, Roland. Always. A girl from one of our friendly packs is missing, and the goddamn South Cliffs probably had something to do with it. Going after them isn't just my opinion, it's the goddamn rules. The traditions."

He was smart enough to recognize that she meant business.

"You did go out of your way to help me," he observed. "And I wouldn't want anything to happen to that girl, even though I don't know her. But frankly, I'm not a member of—"

"You're my boyfriend, remember?" she interjected. "Or at least, that's what everyone thinks until further notice, so as long as we're practically mated, you *are* pack. The rest will accept you because *I've* accepted you."

By now, she'd gunned it out of the parking lot and down the road in the direction she'd seen the atrocious white SUV going.

To soften her words, she smiled at him, and not in a clever or amused way; this was different. It must have worked because she saw him melt. Suddenly, he was on board with the program just because it would keep him by her side.

"All right," he almost whispered. "Let's get the bastards."

"That's what I wanted to hear." She gave him a soft punch on the arm. "Besides, we'll be able to keep you away from the witches. Can't be any safer than with a bunch of werewolves who'll rip anyone who messes with them to shreds. Well, one, at least."

He reacted to her punch by aiming his index finger toward her ear and slowly moving it closer. She swatted his hand away.

Roland adjusted his jacket. "Those wolves will rip *me* to shreds if I can't belt-nunchaku them into oblivion this time. We won't have the home-field advantage, you realize."

Bailey ran a yellow light and changed lanes to avoid a forced turn, cutting in front of the car behind her, who honked. She was getting the hang of city driving.

As for Roland's comment, she didn't want him to end up as meat scraps, but...

"Hey," she said. "If you do get dismembered, disemboweled, and decapitated, at least Shannon and her color-coordinated groupies won't be able to use you for a sperm donor."

He let out a low, awkward laugh. "I can't argue with that logic."

An hour and a half had passed—a delightful interlude filled with asshole drivers in annoying vehicles.

"No, listen," Roland insisted. "The fact that they were heading east doesn't mean they were going to continue east, because then they'd end up driving their horrible flame-decaled SUV straight into the frickin' Columbia River. That would be nice for everyone else, but I doubt even they are that stupid. Now, from what G-Maps is telling me, there are a few winding back roads that go off into the hills, but somehow, that doesn't seem right."

"Bullshit," Bailey retorted, braking hard to avoid a lane-change by some asshole in a Tesla ahead of her. "Some of us are used to back roads through the hills. Seems like exactly the kind of place they'd head for."

They hit a stalemate, neither being exactly furious with the other, but both frustrated by their long search. They'd been all over the northern and eastern areas of Portland by now, with no results.

"I mean," Roland went on, "there's also Veterans Memorial Highway. That follows the river, but it would take them pretty far afield—toward southeast Washington. I dunno, somehow I think they just have some kind of business in the city, and when they're done, they're probably planning to head back to Greenhearth, or at least somewhere in your neck of the woods. In other words, we have to eliminate the city as a possibility. Then we can look at trailing them to the mountains."

Bailey tried not to roll her eyes. "We already combed a lot of the city. They're probably halfway down the Cascades by now."

"Well, it only takes them being one block away for us not to see them. The whole reason we came to Portland was to lose ourselves, remember? That also applies to anyone we might be trying to track down."

He was sort of right, but it wasn't like she would admit that aloud.

"Whatever," she grumbled. "We'll go through this last suburb to the south. What's it called?"

"Gresham," he informed her.

She took a right turn, not expecting any more success than they'd already had. In other words, none.

The wizard ran a hand through his hair; she had noticed that was a habit of his. It was straight and lanky, so he could get away with washing it every day without it going to frizz the way Bailey's would. Men had all the luck.

"This," he muttered, "is really getting tiresome. And frankly, I shouldn't be sticking my neck out. We've already tried our best."

"Hey!" she protested. "I saved your ass, and now it's *my* ass on the line since I can't fail my pack."

He put his feet up on her dashboard. "So my ass is forfeit too, is it? Well, if you want it, it's all yours."

Words failed her for a moment, and blood rushed to her face, inflaming her cheeks. She had *not* expected a comeback like that.

But before she could come up with some clever way to punish him for his boldness, he retracted his feet and again started playing what looked like a vigorous game of pocket pool.

Her spirits sank.

"Shit," he almost snarled. "The coin. It's going crazy again. We need to—"

Bailey jerked the wheel to the right, fish-tailing the

truck onto a perpendicular street and narrowly avoiding a car stopped at the intersection.

"Fuckin' hell," she gasped. "That was *them*. Opposite direction."

The silver Jaguar had appeared from seemingly out of nowhere, turning off the same road they'd been navigating and now heading away from them down the other side of the cross street.

And this time, unlike with Oberlin's Suburban, she had seen the driver—a slender young woman with fuchsia hair.

Roland had tensed and shut up once the car swerved, but now he was looking over his shoulder.

"Christ, it was. Good reflexes. Two more seconds and they would have spotted us. Uh, let's see—they're still driving. Wait, fuck, they stopped. But, uh…nope, they're not coming this way. And the coin is calming down."

He blew air from his lungs and stared at her. "You saved my ass again. Nicely done. I take back everything bad I ever said about you, except the thing about my ass just now. That stands."

A goofy smile spread over her face as she took another turn deeper into the suburbs. "Yeah, yeah, don't mention it. You're gonna pay for that last part, though."

She was driving faster than she knew she should— about thirty-five miles per hour in what was obviously a residential twenty-five zone. But there didn't seem to be any cops around, and she wanted to get the hell away from the witches with all due haste.

With that in mind, she made another turn, again taking them west.

"I wonder," she mused, "what the hell they were doing,

going east like that. Maybe they figured we were literally heading for the hills."

"Probably," Roland agreed. He seemed flustered—not just with the immediate situation, but today in general. There was still a kind of laid-back confidence about him that Bailey couldn't stop herself from admiring, but with his complaining and general attitude recently, the whole ordeal seemed to be taking its toll on him.

Bailey felt the adrenaline surge. Their ordeal was about to get even more interesting.

About an intersection and a half ahead of them, standing out like the sorest thumb in the Pacific Northwest, was an abomination—a lifted white SUV with blue and purple flames along the sides and rear.

"Roland," Bailey said as her foot pressed down on the gas, "I guess you were right last night after all, and so was everyone else. I really *am* a magnet for trouble."

He glanced quickly from her face to the windshield, peering through it. "Oh, no. Nothing fails like success, I suppose. Hoo, boy!"

Bailey gunned it.

The Tundra's engine roared as the cylinders fired, the speedometer's needle rising to forty-five, then fifty. Bailey ran a red light. The SUV was still a ways ahead, but it was getting closer.

"What the hell?" Roland grated. "Slow down! Shit, we already spotted them, okay? We're not going to lose them at this distance."

"Oh, yes, we are," Bailey insisted, "if we get stuck at a red light. No way to know which way they turned. And they haven't spotted us yet. If we nail 'em now, we can wrap this whole thing up in a few minutes."

A few residents shouted and waved fists as Bailey's truck rocketed past. Another light appeared in front of them, turned yellow, and then shifted to red just before it passed overhead.

"Bailey," Roland countered, "getting pulled over will waste a *lot* more time than sitting at a light."

"Fuck it," she said.

The wizard threw up his hands. "You don't get it, do you? This isn't your little Podunk town. The cops here aren't going to just slap your wrist and turn a blind eye. They don't know you. In fact, you're an outsider, which will only make them more suspicious and hostile. Jesus. Not to mention, you could run over someone's kid. *That'd* be a great fucking thing to do while we're trying to save a little girl, wouldn't it? Think. You're acting like a crazy—"

He stopped, biting off his final word.

It was, of course, "bitch," but he thought better of it. Having her attempt to kick his ass while simultaneously engrossed in a psycho driving spree would get both of them killed.

Bailey was beyond the point of caring what he said right now, though. Her total focus was on running Dan Oberlin's vehicle into the ground.

Fortunately, the SUV hit a red light half a block ahead of them and came to a stop.

"Okay, there, see?" Roland pointed out. "We'll just be, like, two cars behind them. Now hold on a sec. I can whip up an enchantment that will let us track them. Then you won't *need* to drive like you're desperate for a tour of the local jail."

She took a deep breath. "Okay, but it better work. I *won't* lose them, not now."

Roland produced a penny from his pocket and leaned over it, mumbling something inaudible and flexing his fingers in odd ways. Midway into the process, he poked her arm.

"The hell was that?" she asked.

He didn't reply since he was hurrying to complete the spell. They'd rolled to a stop by now, with another SUV and a sedan separating them from the white Suburban.

"Okay," the wizard told her. "Trust me on this."

He rolled down his window, leaned out, and tossed the penny. He lobbed it gently enough that by rights, it should have plunked to the ground a few feet away, but somehow the little piece of copper followed a curving path all the way to the back of Oberlin's vehicle, then planted itself right on his bumper and stayed there.

Bailey blinked. "Shit. Nice job, wiz kid."

The light turned green.

"Thanks." He shrugged. "Watch for the trail of light it leaves. Only you and I can see it; that was why I touched you there. It will stick around for about an hour, so we'll have plenty of time to stay on their trail the legal, safe, *sane* way, even if they get out of our visual range."

Bailey accelerated, staying a reasonable distance behind, and to her mild amazement, she noticed a faint beam of green light hovering above the road, emanating from the back of the Suburban like bizarre semi-frozen exhaust. It looked like a rainbow, minus the other six colors.

"Well, I'll be damned," she remarked.

They drove for about a mile, until the other SUV turned into a driveway, leaving only the sedan between them and the hideous Suburban. Roland relaxed now that Bailey was driving the speed limit.

Her arms and hands trembled with tension. She still wanted to just run them down, but that would be stupid at this point. The faint green beam of light would guide them where they needed to go.

After another mile, Oberlin turned right, while the sedan behind him kept going straight. Bailey slowed down and put her right blinker down. Then she followed at a slightly greater distance.

"Ok," Roland murmured, "good. Might be wise to let them get a little ahead of us, maybe pick up another tail-gater or two to block us from their sight."

"Yeah," Bailey replied, failing to hide her impatience, "that's the idea. I know what I'm doing."

They fell farther behind after a four-way stop, and a blue convertible pulled out behind the Suburban. Its roof was up, but it was still low enough that some of the black Tundra would be visible if Oberlin or his cronies looked hard enough. Better than nothing, though.

For almost twenty minutes, they followed the lifted SUV's rambling, arbitrary path through the eastern suburbs, then back into the northern part of the city.

Roland fidgeted in his seat. "Christ, they're moving west, so they must not be ready to return home yet. Are they going all the way to the goddamn coast?"

"*Wherever* they're going," Bailey said darkly, "we're tracking them down." The weird green light-trail continued to guide her. "Even if they bear north and go all the way to Seattle or fucking Alaska, we're *finding* those girls."

"By now," Roland stated, "I know when not to bother arguing with you."

They approached a major intersection near the junction with the expressway. Suddenly the blue convertible turned into a gas station, and they found themselves right behind the Suburban, sitting at a red light.

"Shit," Bailey muttered. "Try not to, I dunno, look at them too hard and draw their attention."

Even as she said this, her eyes were wandering to the vehicle's rear window. Through it, she could make out four dark, shaggy heads. The one behind the wheel was higher than the others and hatefully familiar. She had definitely not made a mistake in identifying either the truck or its driver.

As she pulled her gaze away, it got stuck on the rearview mirror—where Dan Oberlin's face was looking right at her.

"Uh-oh," she exhaled.

"What?" asked Roland. "Did they—"

Tires squealed and a puff of dirty smoke erupted in front of their windshield as Dan slammed his foot on the gas, his SUV rocketing through the red light, causing two cars to swerve and honk as he made straight for the expressway ramp just past the intersection.

Bailey's eyes bulged. "*Motherfucker!*" Her foot descended.

Roland smacked himself in the face as the black pickup blasted into the intersection behind the Suburban and his phone went flying. The traffic light was still red as they went under it, the merging ramp growing in size to engulf them as they entered it.

"It's curved," he warned her. "It loops around, and then you need to speed up once you're on the expressway. You—ohhh, shit!"

The vehicle tilted and skidded as Bailey navigated the ramp at fifty-five or sixty, well above the speed limit, though at least that meant she was already about up to speed for what lay ahead. Oberlin's SUV was already barreling down the freeway.

Bailey merged easily, cutting off another motorist who braked and veered into the other lane, and then things were little more than chaos. The girl had never driven on this type of road before, but she grasped the general idea quickly enough, accelerating to eighty as she wove between cars, trying to catch up to the Suburban.

Roland pointed in front of them. "It's still leaving a trail, see? You don't have to do this. We can just track it."

"It's fainter," Bailey said. "Must not work as well when they speed up. I can barely see the damn thing, and if they get too far ahead, they'll have time to stash the goddamn truck somewhere, flee on foot, and maybe tell someone we're after them, so we get ambushed by twenty assholes as soon as we stop."

Groaning, the wizard conceded, "You do *kinda* have a point there."

CHAPTER TWELVE

As the werewolves' SUV barreled forward in its mad dash to escape them, other cars started to realize crazy shit was happening and started to jerk their wheels to the right, haphazardly pulling over to the shoulder to avoid a rear-end collision with two consecutive trucks.

Bailey felt a giddy rush of excitement and terror. Her hands and shoulders trembled, yet her mind was focused and coherent. She'd never driven this fast before since Greenhearth didn't have the roads for it. Trees and buildings and other cars whizzed past in a blur.

Roland closed his eyes. "We're gonna get reported to the Highway Patrol. I'll see if I can at least obscure our license plate. Shoulda done that a while ago."

He raised his hands and slowly contorted them as if kneading dough.

"You do that," Bailey agreed.

No police appeared for the next minute, though, as they veered around a curved part of the road, the wheels leaving the pavement for a second. It was all Roland could do to maintain concentration on his spell.

Then Oberlin braked, swerved right, and cut in front of another car to shoot down an exit ramp, disappearing from the freeway altogether.

"No!" Bailey barked. She tried to get over, but a semi-truck, honking furiously, appeared and blocked her path. There was no way she could make it to the exit in time without totaling her Tundra.

"Keep going," Roland advised, emerging from the depths of whatever cloaking magic he'd just cast. "Take the next exit up there—only half a mile. Then head north, and we should intersect their path unless they try to double back on us."

Bailey accelerated again, cut in front of the motorists in the right lane, and slowed down—some—as she took the exit.

"Uh," she asked, "this damn thing is spinning me around again. Which way's north? Wait!"

Ahead and to her left, she saw the Suburban rumbling past, the faint emerald glow still trailing behind it.

She grinned, showing her teeth. "Got 'em. You ain't getting away this time, Dan!"

As they hastened to catch up, Roland pointed out that they were now headed south, much to his surprise.

"They must be planning to cross the river," he suggested.

"We'll burn that bridge when we come to it," said Bailey. "Maybe literally."

Weaving amidst traffic, gunning it when she could to avoid tipping the truck over on sharp turns, Bailey soon came to within about a hundred feet of the SUV, only for Dan to catch sight of her again and floor his gas pedal.

She did likewise. "Shit! Some people don't know when to quit."

Roland gasped. "I know *exactly* what you mean."

Oberlin had to brake to avoid crashing into a lumber truck as he cut through a red light at the intersection ahead. Bailey honked to ensure the people trying to cross the street stayed alert, then followed the Suburban just as the light flicked to green.

Suddenly, they were on a bridge over the Willamette River, just to the south of where they'd crossed it last night after the park.

"Careful!" Roland warned. "We've got *no* room to fuck up here."

"Stuff it," Bailey quipped back. "I know how a bridge works. I'm not *that* much of a hick."

Still, she felt her palms sweating on the wheel and her abdominal muscles clenching.

Ahead, Oberlin sideswiped an unlucky sedan, knocking off its side mirror and scattering glass and debris across the pavement. Bailey gritted her teeth as she piloted the truck toward and then through a narrow gap between two cars on either side, who'd stopped in panic.

"Whoa," Roland exclaimed as they whizzed through, missing the vehicles by a couple of inches each.

Just as unexpectedly as the bridge had appeared, it was gone, and they were back in the city proper.

The white Suburban was gone, too.

"The hell?" Bailey raged. "Where'd he go? Goddammit!"

"The trail," Roland reminded her, pointing. "Over there.

Take a right. Slow down and follow it. There aren't as many places he can go now. Track him the smart way."

She wanted to shout and curse and kick the doorframe, but she refrained since that would do nothing to improve their situation. Instead, she turned right, bringing her speed back down to just over the limit.

Roland spoke again. "Listen to me. Think. He's probably headed into the northwest Industrial district. It's a narrow place between Forest Park and the river, not as maze-like as the eastern suburbs. We can track him easily if he goes there, and if he goes through the park, that reduces his number of paths and will slow him way down."

Shaking her head but recognizing that the wizard was right, Bailey took a deep breath and focused on keeping the barely-visible green light in front of her.

Minutes passed with no sight of the ugly SUV, although as Roland had predicted, they ended up in the northwest corner of town, bearing toward a long row of abandoned-looking buildings arranged close to a wide place in the water.

She leaned forward and squinted. The green trail of light, as near as she could tell, was now gone.

"Shit, Roland," she observed. "Your tracking device crapped out on us, I think."

"It would seem so," he lamented. "They might have had time to remove it, although I don't know how they'd even be aware it was there. More likely, it fell off or got wet when they drove through a puddle or something; water interferes with the spell. Or it might have just stopped. It's supposed to last an hour, but I didn't have enough time to empower the spell to its full potential."

She resisted the urge to drive her fist into the windshield. It wasn't Roland's fault; without the spell, they might have lost Oberlin altogether.

She sighed. "Well, at least we know the general area they're in."

He nodded. "Warehouse district by the piers. Almost cliché, isn't it? I suppose it *is* a convenient place to conduct illegal activity, especially the kinds that are a lot worse than anything *I've* done."

Bailey's jaw muscles tightened. "That's for damn sure."

She pulled the truck behind an empty shed in a weedy lot on the other side of the street. The wizard was on edge, and so was she. Their nervous systems were still keyed up from the car chase, and she half-expected the cops to appear even now.

And they didn't know what they were about to walk into.

"Okay," the girl muttered, "let's just go down the line. They've got to be here, right?"

Roland shrugged. "It's possible they went somewhere else, but I doubt it. And if they did stop here, they're probably not leaving right away. We should have time to search on foot. So yeah."

They climbed out, shutting the doors gently, and darted across the street when it was clear. They headed for a tall hedge, which they promptly crouched behind.

Squinting through a gap in the twisted branches, Bailey mumbled, "I think—yeah, I can see through the window."

"Oh, right," said Roland. "I forgot you have super Were senses. Anything?"

She frowned. "Not really, just a few empty, dusty racks. Cross this one off the list, I think."

Slowly, they crept out from behind the hedge, past the first warehouse and toward the side of the next building. They kept to the shade. They weren't going to any great lengths to sneak around and hide, but it was obvious to them both that it would be best not to blatantly announce their presence.

At least, not yet. When the time came, Bailey wanted Oberlin and the rest of the bastards to know exactly who'd come for them and why. Her right hand rolled itself into a trembling fist.

"What," Roland inquired, "if I might ask, is the plan? I have a few notions of my own, but since pursuing those pricks was your idea, I'll start by asking you."

They half-crouched against the side wall of the warehouse, keeping themselves flat enough to avoid easy detection from the front and below the line of sight of the windows.

"Find them," Bailey stated. "That's Step One. Once we pull that off, Step Two's to charge in, kick ass, and take names. Don't think we need more than two steps. Simplicity is the beauty of the whole thing."

Roland's face was stony. He'd narrowed his eyes and was rolling his tongue around his teeth as he weighed the pros and cons, the dangers and opportunities.

"Eh," he replied, "that might work, although it's not what I had in mind. If we see them before they see us, I should be able to concoct something that will—"

"Oh, come on," she interrupted. She only slightly increased the volume of her voice—it was still a whisper—

but she added a cutting edge to it. "We're already doing more than enough sneaking around if you ask me. I think it's well past time for you to be the big scary badass wizard you *ought* to be."

He stiffened as if someone had thrown something at the back of his head. "What the hell does that mean?" he asked, blinking.

"You're supposedly this powerful magic user, right?" she explained. "I've seen you do a few things that are pretty impressive, but mostly you just keep running away, or hiding, or trying not to deal with things directly. Right now, you're trying not to get into a fight with a few werewolves you *already* beat the shit out of."

He grunted low in his throat as they crept toward the rear of the building. "Yes, but we don't know if it's going to be *just* them. The fuckin' Russian Mafia could be in there with ten guys with AKs."

"Well," she shot back, "can't you, like, deflect their bullets back at them or something?"

"In theory." He sighed. "I've never been able to try that one. You know, in the field, in real-time, when the boot hits the grindstone or however the hell the saying goes."

She waved a hand impatiently. "I get the picture. No time like the present to test that shit out, though."

He didn't answer, and as they reached the rear corner, she looked pointedly into his face. "Roland," she began, her voice softer now, "those witches want you *bad*. Even if you hadn't told me, I would have been able to tell once they showed up in the flesh. Women can see these things. Whatever this gift you have is, it's clearly something special."

His eyes stayed locked on hers and widened.

Bailey went on, "Maybe you think that by fleeing from your full potential, you can also get away from them and that other crap you told me about—people just wanting to be near you so your power rubs off on them. But you can't run away from what you *are*. Having power like that, you might as well put it to good use, like helping me save a couple of innocent girls from whatever the hell these assholes have in mind."

The wizard raised the knuckle of his forefinger to the space between his upper lip and his nose, and his eyes went distant.

"Oh," the young woman added, "and don't worry about the moral ramifications or whatever of kicking their butts again, or about how the folks back in Greenhearth— human or Were—might react. These guys aren't good people. They're not well-liked even by the locals in their own town, after all. Daddy Oberlin can buy tolerance, but not respect. Dan and his crew are assholes *at best*, and at worst, they might be goddamn kidnappers."

Roland gave an oddly flippant shrug and loosened up again, regaining some of the swagger she recalled from their first meeting.

"Once again," he stated, "you have a point, I'll admit."

She smiled. "*Several* points, thank you. But good enough; I'll take what I can get. Now let's get those sons of bitches."

He raised an eyebrow at her choice of words, then nodded. Together, they rounded the corner.

Nothing—just weeds, mud, and gravel. Bailey peeked briefly into the rear window, but the warehouse was completely dark within. Nothing suggested anyone was inside, or had been in days or weeks.

"Well, that's a bust," she murmured.

"Onward," Roland said, "to bigger and better things." He gestured toward the next structure, which was half again as large as the one they'd just examined.

They took three steps forward, then stopped dead.

Peeking around the back of the next building was the rear end of a lifted SUV, white and slathered with purple and blue flames.

The werewolf almost whistled. "That settles it."

Moving even more slowly and trying to make no noise, they crossed the short span of open ground and again smashed themselves against the wall beneath the window. They waited there for a few seconds while Bailey listened.

Her eyes widened, and she gestured for Roland to lean closer to her.

"I can hear breathing and movement, plus I can smell them," she said in the softest whisper she could manage.

He nodded, then pointed toward a barely visible door in the side of the warehouse at the back end. He wiggled his fingers and pantomimed opening a lock with a key.

Bailey gave him a thumbs-up and followed him toward the door. Suddenly she didn't feel quite so gung-ho. It wasn't that she was afraid of Dan; it was more that Roland's earlier words about potential heavily armed mobsters waiting in there had begun to sink in.

She stood still as Roland touched the knob, gently turned it, and found it locked. Then he closed his eyes and touched the tip of his index finger to the keyhole. A few seconds later, it clicked faintly, and the door began to move.

Catching his eye, she mouthed, "Let me go first," and crept past him. He waited a few seconds before following.

Within, the building was mostly dark, save for a single naked bulb hanging from the ceiling nearer the front. Here in the back, there were only a few half-rotted wooden shelves, some rusted steel shelves, and a couple of big empty boxes.

Near the front were a few men. Bailey could smell Dan Oberlin among them, but before she examined the group in detail, her attention was drawn to something in the middle of the building, not far beyond where she and the wizard now knelt.

Cages, one against each side wall, big enough that they were probably intended to hold ponies or goats, or maybe large dogs. The cage on the left had four occupants; the one on the right, zero so far. The four in the left-hand cage were young girls ranging in age from about twelve to fifteen, she guessed.

And with absolute certainty, she could say that all the girls were Weres from packs in her region of the Cascades. If not from Greenhearth, then from other nearby towns or isolated homes in the mountains and valleys. Her pulse quickened.

Outside, the pier was close enough that she could hear the water of the river lapping against it, creating just enough interference that she couldn't quite make out what the men up front were saying. On the plus side, that meant any sounds she and Roland might make would be obscured, as well. She just hoped they were too involved to smell her and Roland.

A figure detached itself from the group and came toward them—or rather, toward the cages. It was Dan Oberlin, still wearing his long coat, a small form under each arm.

Bailey's eyes almost bulged out of their sockets. One of the girls was none other than Lauren Heuerman, who, according to Gunney had disappeared last night.

The other was Emma Nimberger, another Greenhearth resident. She must have been the girl from the south side who'd also been taken a couple of days ago, whose name Gunney hadn't been able to recall.

Both were Pack. Both had zip-ties around their wrists and ankles and duct tape over their mouths and they lolled in a stupor—probably drugged, or maybe just exhausted from the long ordeal of their kidnapping.

As Bailey and the wizard watched from the shadows behind a box, Dan deposited the young ladies in the empty cage to the right, bringing the total up to six prisoners between the two enclosures. He shut and locked the door, then strode back up front to talk things over with the rest of the group.

By now, Bailey's eyes were better adjusted to the dim light, and she was over the initial shock of seeing the girls. She studied the figures at the other end of the building.

Predictably, Oberlin had three of his minions with him —Chins, the gangly fucker, and the beefy guy whose hand she'd bitten. The redhead wasn't with them, probably thanks to the ankle he'd twisted in Roland's magic mudhole.

In addition to the four South Cliffs, there were also three tall, bearded men in clean dark brown suits. Bailey had no idea who they were. They *might* have been Weres, but she'd have had to get closer to smell them in order to tell. They might also have been ordinary humans.

She turned to Roland and breathed, "Hey, do you have a spell that can, uh, amplify them? I can't hear."

"Way ahead of you," he responded just as quietly, closing his eyes and making a motion with his right hand as though drawing a string closer to them.

Five seconds later, the conversation among the men was abruptly as clear as though Bailey were standing three feet away from it.

"...reasonable price, since we might be looking to resell them," one of the suited men was saying. "We'll probably keep *some*, but other packs will clearly be interested."

Dan grunted. "We just quoted you a reasonable price. Lot of risk to us, you know. We gotta make a goddamn profit here, and like you said, there are other people interested. Birth rates are so low that we can afford to wait for the highest bidder."

Bailey's skin crawled as it all came together in her head.

Throughout the Were community, there was occasional yet pervasive grumbling about how their people were having fewer children. Their ancient mating traditions were not working well in the modern world. Things were changing.

The pressure she had been subjected to was part of it. Female werewolves of fertile age, even if just barely, were highly prized. It was only a matter of time before some scumbag thought to try to sell teenage girls into forced marriages, allowing packs to grow their numbers at the cost of anything resembling basic decency, let alone legality.

A red haze of shuddering rage began to fill her, beginning in her brain and spreading to every part of her body.

"So, then," the wizard breathed. "That's it. It's just as bad as we feared it might be."

"Yes," Bailey almost growled through her now-clenched teeth. "*It is.*"

Roland nodded and spoke again hurriedly before she could do anything.

"I'm not going to try to dissuade you from launching a rescue right here and now. That would be pointless since I know you that well already, but there's some stuff we have to think about. Like, for example, if the fight goes badly for us, we might not be able to get out safely with the girls. The last thing we want is to get ourselves killed or captured without saving any of them."

Bailey turned her eyes to his, and an unexpected rush of emotion hit her, briefly eclipsing her anger. He *cared*—about her, and about the young Weres they were here to help. She was almost ashamed of assuming he was cowardly earlier. Really, he was just trying to be sensible so they'd be more likely to succeed.

She gave a slow nod. "Yeah, good point. So what do you suggest?"

His mouth twisted in a strange way. "I'm going to give you a number and I want you to text it, saying exactly where we are."

She squinted, wondering if he had friends in high

places he hadn't told her about yet. "Uh, okay. Whose number is it? And why can't you send it?"

Now the expression on his face started to make sense—it was a mixture of resignation, impatience, and amusement.

"My phone's still in the truck. And it's Shannon's."

Bailey bit her tongue and clapped a hand over her mouth to keep from bursting out with a barrage of profanity that might give them away. After she swallowed her initial outburst, she lowered her hand.

"*What?* Why the hell should we contact *her?*"

She went cold for a moment, afraid Roland might be aiming to barter with the witches—their help in exchange for his body.

He seemed to sense her train of thought, and his demeanor shifted back to warm and reassuring.

"As a diversion. We've got a lot of werewolves here, and the guys in the suits might have guns. And we have half a dozen girls to bust out of cages; that's a lot of work to do. Why not allow ourselves to focus just on the girls by leading a trio of powerful, unpleasant, pissed-off witches onto a collision course with our furry asshole friends here? I mean, you were right, we can't call the cops since this is a supernatural matter."

A slow smile spread across her face. "Roland, you're a genius after all. Not bad." She pulled out her phone as he gave her the number.

"Just, uh," he instructed, "say something like you're through with me and she can have me. You know, like you're telling her woman to woman that I pissed you off and now you'll collaborate with them against me. Girls do shit like that all the time, don't they?"

Bailey frowned. "Some do. I don't, but yeah, I get the idea." She typed in an appropriate message, mentioning that they were in the third warehouse in the northwest pier district, then tapped Send.

Roland chuckled very softly. "I'm sure they'll be here *very* soon."

"Probably," she agreed, recalling the insane jealousy, envy, and possessiveness that had practically oozed off the three sorceresses. She wasn't much looking forward to seeing them again, even though they and Oberlin's gang might send each other to hell, or at least to jail or the hospital.

Bailey turned toward the cage with the four girls. "I'm going to video this so we have— Fuck!"

Roland frowned. "What's wrong?"

"No space on my phone. Well, the girls' testimony will just have to do. After we get them out of here."

In the chaos that was no doubt about to erupt, they just might be able to pull off this little rescue mission. *Maybe.*

CHAPTER THIRTEEN

The South Cliffs and the three business mobster types wandered closer to the front doors. All of them now either had their backs turned, or were blocked from sight of where Bailey and Roland were.

Better still, they weren't looking at the cages.

Bailey inhaled. "Let's get this show on the road. We can probably free at least a couple of them before your girlfriends show up and crash the party."

"Aye," Roland agreed. "But be careful. We don't want them to find us beforehand."

The young woman didn't stop to acknowledge his words, but she nodded. She'd succeeded at getting him to be more proactive, and it was only fair that she accept his advice about doing things the smart way.

She crawled toward the cage on the left. Her instinct was to make for the other one since that was where Lauren and Emma were—girls she knew from her own pack and town—but it made more sense to start with the enclosure that was easier to reach.

The wizard followed her. For his part, he was contemplating how best to get the cages open—whether to magically open the doors or to melt through the bars at the rear. The former might make noise. The latter would create light. Neither was perfect.

But luck was on their side in one regard: the wind outside had picked up and was sloshing the Willamette roughly against the pier, creating enough ambient racket that they'd have to do something really stupid to be heard.

Bailey reached the edge of the cage and rolled toward the wall to allow Roland to examine it. He did, thinking quickly.

During the brief inspection, two of the girls turned their eyes toward them. They seemed aware of the pair's presence but didn't react; their gazes were dull. Sedated, Bailey concluded.

"Okay," the Seattleite whispered, "I should be able to heat up the bars enough to bend them aside in the rear here and then slip the girls out one at a time. It will only take a couple minutes. You can lead them back to the door."

"Sure thing," Bailey agreed.

Roland licked his lips and rubbed his forefingers together, almost the way a person might rub two sticks to start a fire. A soft red glow appeared on his hands, and Bailey suddenly worried that their foes might see it. Nothing happened, though.

The wizard then gripped two adjacent bars, holding onto them to transfer the magical heat energy and pulling in opposite directions as they began to glow. The metal rods softened and moved gradually apart. One of the girls retracted her foot to avoid being burned. They weren't totally insensate, then.

After Roland removed his hands, the bars cooled and darkened. He waited for a moment and then tapped the metal to ensure it wasn't hot enough to cause harm. He also checked the size of the gap. Should be big enough for teenagers to squeeze through.

He reached through the bars, grabbed the nearest girl's ankle—fortunately they weren't zip-tied like the new arrivals—and pulled her toward the gap with one hand. With the other, he raised a finger to his lips to remind her to be quiet. She didn't protest.

As he and Bailey moved the girl out, the negotiations up front continued.

"…that one. She's supposedly a slut at the high school, which ought to increase—"

"No," one of the businessmen interrupted, "that will decrease her value. You have to consider the traditional values some people hold."

Trying to ignore them, Bailey helped the first prisoner crawl toward the back door. It wasn't hard since the girl was waking up from her drugged stupor and seemed to grasp what was going on.

She and Roland emptied the first cage within the next couple of minutes. They had the first three girls wait by the back door in silence, telling them they could flee if things went south, but otherwise, to wait for their rescuers to escort them.

The wizard and the werewolf returned to the cage and helped the last girl out. She was the most out of it of the four, and they pretty much had to carry her.

Now, finally, they all stood by the door. The South Cliffs and their customers hadn't noticed anything amiss yet. Roland slung the fourth girl over his shoulder and stepped quickly out the door as Bailey urged the other three behind him.

"Damn," the wizard commented, "I almost can't believe that worked."

They hustled back the way they'd come, around the pier-facing sides of the first two warehouses before running across the street to Bailey's truck in the opposite lot. Roland laid the semi-conscious girl in the cab while the other three piled into the truck bed and laid down flat.

One of them, a skinny freckle-faced redhead, gestured at the road with her head and then looked at the pair with intense eyes.

"Yes," Bailey told her, "we're going to get you out of here, but not just yet. We have to go back for the others. Those two are from my hometown. Can't just leave them. We'll be back in a jiffy. Just lie here quietly and wait, okay?"

The girl clearly didn't like the idea, and for a moment, it looked like she might cry.

Roland stepped in. "Everything will be all right. We'll just be a minute. They don't even know we sprung the four of you yet."

He and Bailey scuttled back to the warehouse, moving as fast as they could at first, then slowing to keep the noise down as they approached the small rear door again.

Roland sighed as they crawled back into the dim structure. "This is going to be harder, you realize," he pointed out. "We'll have to creep across a semi-well-lit area in the middle of the floor to reach the cage, or else climb over a bunch of shelving that will probably collapse as soon as we touch it."

"Hell or high water," Bailey replied, "we're bringing those girls home."

"Agreed," said the wizard. "Just don't be shocked if things start to—"

Just then, with them about to try to cross the middle space, Roland stopped. Bailey glanced at him and saw him clutch his pants pocket.

"Oh, shit!" she lamented very quietly.

The warehouse's front door, along with the entire front wall, exploded. It didn't merely blast apart; a fireball grew out of a bright purple flash before changing to normal orange flames, which licked around the ragged edges of the blast hole.

The South Cliffs and the three guys in suits had all staggered back. Chins had fallen on his ass, and it looked like one of the businessmen was bleeding from a cut on his forearm where a flying piece of debris had snagged him. Even Bailey and Roland, far from the entrance, had felt the ripple of force and the wave of heat.

Bailey gawked for a second, even though she knew she shouldn't. "Have to admit," she mumbled, "they know how to make a good entrance."

"True," Roland acceded.

Three figures stomped in through the smoke, ignoring the shattered remains of the door beneath their feet.

"All right," Shannon DiGrezza demanded, not bothering to use her silky voice, just leaping straight to the shrill, jagged one, "where the *fuck* is Roland? We know he's here!"

"The hell?" one of the werewolves shot back, spittle flying from his mouth in agitated confusion.

One of the three men in suits—he seemed to be their leader—stepped forward. "We never heard of nobody named Roland. Who the hell are you?"

"*Bullshit!*" Callie McCluskey yelled, jumping forward a step and extending a finger. "His stupid little wannabe-girlfriend just tattled on him. He's here!"

Aida Nassirian raised her purse from hip-level to stomach-level. "It is okay," she cooed. "We won't hurt him. *Much.*"

The head suit jerked, almost as if he'd been slapped. "Did you bitches just threaten me? Do you have any idea who we are? You just busted into the wrong fucking warehouse!"

He reached into his jacket, and in a flash, produced a big semiautomatic pistol. One of his companions pulled out a similar gun, and the other whipped out a sawed-off shotgun.

During the confrontation, the pair of rescuers had scampered to the back of the other cage. Roland was already melting through the bars.

"Wooo," he almost whistled. "This is *bad*. We need to get the hell out of here ASAP." He yanked on the metal rods, bending them aside as Lauren and Emma, having been jolted to attention by the explosion, tried not to panic.

"No shit, Sherlock," said Bailey. She wriggled forward to grab Lauren's shoulders and the wizard yanked on the hem of her pants. Roland pulled her out through the bars, which were still almost warm enough to burn and just barely warped enough for the girl to squeeze through.

As they started to repeat the process for Emma, the deafening cracks of gunshots in an enclosed space split the air, and there was another purple flash. Between it all, Bailey heard the familiar bestial growling of Weres who had just shifted form.

Lauren screamed behind the tape, but the gunshots drowned out the sound. Bailey sprang to her feet to embrace the girl and drag her behind a crate. Roland appeared with Emma a couple of seconds later, and they got the zip-ties off their ankles and the duct tape off their mouths.

Glancing over her shoulder, Bailey saw one of Oberlin's boys—Gangly, she was pretty sure—in wolf form, light brown fur bristling as foaming drool trailed from his fangs. A silvery-fuchsia orb of light came toward him and he narrowly leapt clear of it as it crashed into the wall, sending a sonic pulse across half the warehouse and warping and cracking the wood and metal and plaster.

Bailey's head snapped toward Roland and she whispered, "We need to get them out of here. At least back to the truck, while I—or we—put a stop to this fuckery."

"Agreed," Roland replied. Bailey handed Lauren to him, and he led the girls toward the door.

She followed a few steps behind, trying to ignore the gunshots, curses, snarls, crackles, and whooshes. Shannon's increasingly unhinged and horrifying screams of frustration were the worst noises of all, though.

Another violet flash of light, and a shapeshifted werewolf—small but tubby, probably Chins—flew between the now-empty cages, smashing through a decrepit shelving unit and scattering its pieces.

"Crap!" Bailey exclaimed. She raised her arms to keep the debris from hitting Roland and the girls.

The werewolf sprang to his feet. Rather than spin toward the witches, though, he looked at Bailey.

The lupine growl that emerged from his thick, meaty throat somehow formed into a parody of human speech.

"Youuuu," he grated.

That was it. Bailey was no longer the slightest bit interested in sneaking out and running away without a fight. She felt like she'd been struck by a bolt of lightning, only for it to invigorate her instead of killing her.

"*Fuckin' A, it's me!*" she roared. She charged forward, and her fist crashed into the wolf's snout. He yelped and fell back, although his claws were already lashing toward her, forcing her to pivot to the side. Then she tackled him into the pile of broken materials.

"Hey!" a male voice bellowed from somewhere up front. "What the hell is going on back there! Check it out!"

"*What?*" Shannon howled. "*He* must be back there! Callie, stop them!"

Roland had by now reached the door and opened it. He was about ready to throw up, not only from the general violence, but also because Bailey had let herself get drawn into it. He needed to get the girls to safety posthaste and then save her.

He looked the teens in the eyes. "Go to our truck," he instructed them. "It's a black pickup—lifted—parked across the street that way. The other girls are already there, and they'll help you. We'll be out soon, I promise!"

Nodding, Lauren and Emma darted out the door. Unwisely, they moved in a straight line rather than ducking behind the other warehouses, but at least they'd reach the Tundra sooner.

Roland slammed the door and spun back toward the melee.

The witches and the other werewolves had interfered with each other's efforts to check the back of the warehouse, so there was that.

Bailey, meanwhile, was wrestling a fat wolf-creature and slowly losing, although it impressed the shit out of him that she was putting up a good fight against such a monster. Even in human form, she was one hell of a Were.

"All right," he ground out, pulling his belt free of his pants. "Looks like I need to teach this prick the same lesson all over again."

The two girls ran. They were trying not to panic, but were confused and terrified. They understood on some primal level that this was the kind of situation in which there were good people who wanted to help them. If they did what they were told, they might have a chance.

They didn't know who the handsome blond man was, but he'd been with Bailey, so he must have been on their side.

Then again, Lauren Heuerman had grown up believing that all Weres were on the same side. Despite the old rivalries between the different packs, there was a sense that they were all family in a way. She'd assumed that if anyone hurt her, it would be a human.

But no, a group of Weres from Greenhearth had

snatched her from the side of the road as she walked home —the South Cliffs. Nobody liked them much, but she'd never thought they would…

"There!" Emma cried out. "The black truck."

They picked up their pace, briefly checking the road for traffic before they sprinted across it. Three teenage girls—Weres, all of them—suddenly sat up in the truck's open bed.

"Hey!" one of them called. "It's the new ones. Over here!"

As they practically jumped into the truck, Lauren cast a glance over her shoulder toward the warehouse, where a battle had broken out.

Smoke, screams, crackling explosions, and flashes of light erupted from the blown-apart front of the building. From time to time, a dark figure streaked past what little of the opening she could see. Werewolves growled, and the three strange and terrifying women who'd burst in kept shouting in weird voices that reminded her of the cawing of crows. She shuddered.

"Get in!" one of the girls urged.

Lauren ran to the truck, then jumped and grabbed the bed rail. The others seized her arms and shirt and helped her in.

Once she was safely amongst them, she decided to report what the blond man had said. "They're coming." She rubbed her eyes; her head still felt woozy from whatever Dan Oberlin had shot her full of. "They just have to, uh, take care of something first."

She swallowed, and on the faces of the other five

teenagers, she could clearly read the question that was in her own mind.

Could even *Bailey* handle something like this?

225

Roland's belt lashed out, moving faster than even the werewolf's eye could follow, snapping at angles nature should not have allowed. Even in wolf form, his enemy still had an interesting collection of chins.

The leather strap raked across them, drawing blood from his lips, loosening a fang, and striking his wet canine nose for good measure. He yelped and tried to spring away, but Bailey had looped her arms under his front legs and was holding him firm.

"Good shot," she complimented the wizard. "Now kick him really hard in the balls or the stomach or something."

"Comin' right up," he assured her. He stepped forward and his foot flashed out, at first seeming to go high for the abdomen. When the werewolf raised his leg to block, the foot shot lower and connected with Chins' fur-covered groin.

The werewolf's growl of rage turned into a low, sickening groan.

"Nice," said Bailey. She retracted her arms, then

launched a fist into the side of the beast's head, splitting open the skin of her knuckles but driving his skull into another of the half-collapsed shelves. It made a satisfying *thunk*, and Chins collapsed to the floor, unconscious.

They moved toward each other, laughing, but there was no time.

Any victory celebration would have been short-lived anyway since squeaking sneakers were moving their way. They pivoted toward the sound.

Caldoria had managed to break through the line of werewolves to investigate what was going on in the rear of the building. The short blonde girl stopped where she was the instant she saw Roland. Her eyes bulged, and her mouth stretched open.

"No, you don't," the wizard snapped and made a throwing motion at her face.

Bailey saw a faint distortion in the air but no object. Nonetheless, the witch's head reared back, and she made a gulping, choking noise as though something was stuck in her mouth.

"Hah!" Bailey laughed and balled up her fists. "I'll take care of the rest."

She charged.

Roland started. "Wait! No!"

Unfortunately, Callie was only using one hand to grip her throat as she tried to overcome the spell. With the other, she made a backhanded motion toward Bailey. A flash of light the same shade of blue as the witch's jacket winked out of the darkness and instantly solidified, smacking Bailey aside as surely as if she'd run into a pane of double-thick glass.

"*Oof!*" she grunted as she toppled, hitting the floor hard and rolling into the wall.

Roland stepped in to engage the witch before she could do any more harm. By now, Callie had managed to spit out the invisible object choking her, but Roland still had the advantage.

He raised his arms sharply upward, palms facing toward him, fingers straight up, and a portion of the concrete floor burst out of its place beneath the witch's feet. Bailey, groaning and climbing to her knees, watched with a mixture of fascination and glee.

The dislodged section of floor catapulted the loud-mouthed fair-haired woman into the air. She screamed and her limbs flailed, but one of her hands pointed straight at Roland.

"Shiiiiit," he exclaimed as he began to slide backward on his heels as though someone were pushing him. He none-theless swiped his arm toward the airborne witch and hit her with another invisible wave of force.

Callie, raving and sputtering, was knocked out of her initial trajectory and plummeted earthwards at an angle, crashing into both Dan Oberlin and one of the brown-suited guys, who had caught up with her. They sprawled to the floor, even as they struggled against Shannon's and Aida's magic.

Despite the ongoing fight, Bailey cracked up. Then she remembered Roland.

She jumped to her feet, gritting her teeth in pain since Caldoria's spell had banged her up pretty good. Then she bolted for Roland, who was trying to undo the spell that had him speeding toward the metal shelves against the back wall of the warehouse.

Focusing on his feet, he managed to slow himself down, but he couldn't stop. It also seemed like his feet were fixed to the floor; he could not simply step out of the spell or jump to the side.

The slowdown was all the time Bailey needed. She bolted toward him, then past and behind him, wrapping her hands around his waist and trying to heave him toward the back door.

"Bailey!" the wizard gulped. "That won't work. I'm locked into—*Fuck!*"

She discovered that the hard way as he jerked her off her feet and carried them both toward the wall. At least the extra weight slowed him down to walking speed.

He gestured wildly. "I've almost got it!"

"I sure hope so!" she exclaimed, trying to regain her footing even as she dragged on him to further reduce his speed.

Suddenly, he stopped. Bailey, pulling on him, stumbled back and almost fell again, but managed to brace herself against a crate. Then both of them stood, frozen except for the labored motions of their breathing.

Bailey spoke first. "Okay, then. Let's book it."

Callie's obnoxious voice filled the entire structure. "Roland's back there! That little bitch is still with him! She tricked us!"

"And," another voice added; Bailey was pretty sure it belonged to Chins, who must have regained consciousness by now, "the cages are empty! They sprung the girls!"

Roland cleared his throat. "*Hustle.*"

He didn't need to tell her twice.

They barreled through the back door fast and hard enough to knock it off its hinges, and then both sprinted as fast as humanly possible toward the back of the second warehouse, cutting between it and the first. This took them directly toward the Tundra while keeping a building between them and the guns and magic spells.

As they crossed the street, the welcoming committee emerged from the destroyed front of the third warehouse. There were a couple of cars passing by, however, and they seemed reluctant to open fire, either with pistols or weird blasts of colored light.

Instead, they made for their vehicles. The three witches climbed swiftly into Shannon's Jaguar, while the South Cliffs piled into Dan's Suburban. The three business types, strangely, had stopped on the other side of the street and were stripping off their coats.

There were now two girls in the cab with them, and Bailey noted that the rest of the rescued girls had arranged themselves in the truck's bed and were trying to tie themselves in with a length of rope she kept back there. It probably wouldn't work, but it was better than nothing.

Something sank inside her at the prospect of having to outrun two different vehicles with a bunch of kids in the back. This was not going to be easy.

Roland seemed to read her mind as they hopped into the cab. "I'll whip up something to keep them from falling out," he said. For some reason, he had scooped up a bunch of rocks and gravel in his arms, and now he deposited the pile on the seat between him and the sixth girl. "You just focus on—"

The engine roared to life almost the instant she put the key in the ignition.

"Well," he remarked, "*that* was fast." He strapped himself into his seat.

"What," asked Bailey, "you thought my motor wouldn't perk up when I needed it to? What kinda mechanic do you take me for?"

She was already gunning it south.

Behind them, they could see the Jaguar and the Suburban converging on the street at the same time. They were still a ways back, but were quickly gaining.

Weirder still, Bailey no longer saw three men in brown suits. Instead, three werewolves had bounded to the sides of the road and were running toward them as fast as the cars were moving.

"I guess they were Weres, after all." She pressed down on the gas.

Roland was caught up in a spell to secure the girls in the truck bed. She just hoped it would work—and that the cops wouldn't find them this time. They'd been damn lucky during the last chase.

Bailey increased her speed, not wanting to get as crazy as she had before, but their pursuers were getting closer. Even the three Weres on foot were closing in. All of them were crazed with the need to recover their quarry—Roland in the case of the witches, and the six girls in the case of the werewolves.

"Okay," the wizard began, "that spell should hold them. Just try not to flip the damn truck. Deal?"

"Deal, obviously," Bailey snapped.

"Great." He ran a hand through his hair. "I think I can

also concoct something that will convince all those asshats to stop following us, so we won't have to pull a repeat of the demolition derby from earlier."

Bailey grimaced. "Ha-ha. Great. Get to it, wiz kid."

"Yes, ma'am." He waved his hands over his pile of pet rocks as the Tundra skidded onto the highway and then crossed a bridge over the Willamette.

Her plan was to bear north and drive along the river, then make for the eastern hills she'd almost driven into earlier when they were looking for Oberlin.

Seeming to perceive her line of thought once again, Roland piped up, "Oh, and don't go north across the Columbia River. That'd put us in Washington State, and if we get caught, it'll technically be a multi-state crime spree, which is *bad*. Might as well keep all your misdeeds in Oregon."

"Thanks for the advice." Behind her, she could see the two hated vehicles keeping pace a hundred or so feet back. The three Weres were still traveling on the road, two on one side, one on the other, knocking aside the occasional astonished pedestrian in their mad dash.

A motorist up ahead swerved, and Bailey saw the driver staring in the mirror at the wolf-beasts. She turned the steering wheel expertly back and forth, weaving around the stalled car. Both the Jaguar and the Suburban had to brake to avoid crashing into it. Horns honked all around.

"Ha, ha!" Bailey scoffed. "None of you pieces of shit can out-drive me. You all just *bought* your rides. I practically *built* this thing!"

Roland didn't respond since he was deep into some arcane process. His eyes actually showed their whites for a moment. Bailey's heart skipped a beat, and she was about to ask if he was okay when he returned to normal.

"Now," he gloated, "let's see how they like the taste of my little gravity bombs. I enchanted them so they'll artificially pick up mass at an exponential rate as they travel through the air, so it'll be like hurling cannonballs at the fuckers."

Bailey blinked. "Clever. Go for it." She pumped the brake as she navigated a sharp curve in the road, veering around a semi and momentarily losing one of the running werewolves.

Roland opened the back window. The girls in the bed stared at him, and he motioned for them to scoot to the sides. Then he gently chucked a pebble toward Shannon DiGrezza's beautiful car.

His aim was a little off, and he'd grabbed one of the smallest stones, so he must have been using it as a test run of the spell. It made a loud whooshing noise and collided heavily with the vehicle's front end, putting a massive dent in the front bumper and stripping off some of the silver paint.

The shrieking of the witches was audible even over the noise of the road.

"Oh, boy." Roland guffawed. "That was almost worth the rest of the shit we've been through today. Now it's that horrible flame-decaled SUV's turn."

Bailey wanted to watch, but she was kind of busy keeping them ahead of their pursuers while trying not to smash into a girder or a storefront.

Before he tossed the next rock, which was closer to the

size of a golf ball, Roland added another piece of commentary.

"It just occurred to me that the witches might be scrambling the police from locking onto us. It's not like all three of them are needed to drive the fucking car, after all, and they're not complete idiots, so drive however you think is best."

"Cool," she growled, and added another five miles per hour to her speedometer.

The wizard pitched the next stone.

This one made a sound like a small mortar as it careened toward the Suburban. It flew high and went straight for the top of the windshield. Dan Oberlin made no effort to dodge; he was probably expecting a spiderweb crack at worst.

Instead, it shattered the glass and tore the entire top off the SUV.

"Whoa!" Roland shouted as the vehicle swerved. The Weres within it cursed and waved their claws and fists.

He then aimed two more stones—one of similar size to the one he'd just thrown and another pebble—toward the Jaguar, but this time, Shannon was ready.

The rocks blasted toward her, but she reached up with a fuchsia-nailed hand and made a sweeping motion with her arm, deflecting them and sending them toward the sides of the street. The smaller one popped the tire of a parked car. The bigger one crumpled an entire railing around it and then disappeared into a hillside in a puff of kicked-up dirt.

"Crap," the wizard muttered. "Well, at least I think we can remove the goddamn werewolves from the equation."

"Yeah," Bailey quipped, "that would help. The Suburban and the assholes on foot. Take 'em out!"

The wolf-beasts bounding alongside the road would catch up to them in about ten seconds, Bailey estimated. She just hoped Roland's throwing arm would be enough to deal with them that quickly.

The wizard took a deep breath, then rapidly pitched five stones in multiple directions, sinking back into deep concentration as he guided the projectiles' course through magic.

The first two struck the front tires of Oberlin's SUV on either side. The awful vehicle leaped into the air as its tires exploded, and frenzied snarls and howls were faintly audible as the rest of the Suburban sailed forward and then slammed into the pavement, kicking up sparks before spinning off the road. It finally crashed into an embankment.

Bailey saw it in her mirrors, and she was torn for a moment between triumphant joy and deep worry. The wolves could have been badly injured, maybe even killed. She saw them moving around before they vanished from sight, though, so they probably weren't dead.

Dan Oberlin and his cronies didn't deserve her sympathy, but she didn't want to celebrate the demise of people she'd known all her life, even if they were the scum of the earth.

The other three rocks zig-zagged in midair as they homed in on the three Weres on foot. The first one landed directly in front of the one on the right side of the road, kicking up earth and sending him tumbling into a sudden muddy hole.

The two on the left were less lucky. The stones hit them in the forelegs, shattering the limbs and causing them to collapse, bellowing in pain even as they unwittingly shifted back into human form.

Roland leaned back and exhaled. "That simplifies matters somewhat."

Bailey nodded sharply, then thought of something. Although the Jaguar was still close behind them, eliminating the wolves had bought them a little bit of breathing space—at least, until the witches started hitting them with magic. Bailey kept one hand on the steering wheel as she slid her phone out of her pocket and speed-dialed Gunney.

The now-damaged silver Jaguar began accelerating, trying to overtake the truck during Bailey's moment of overconfidence.

Shannon gripped the wheel with both hands, the bones standing out against her skin, her eyes blazing, the breeze whipping her purplish hair back from her angular face.

"Dealing with this fuckhead," she hissed, "is almost more trouble than it's worth. When have we ever had to work this goddamn hard just to get laid? If this is his idea of foreplay, it's not working. All he's doing is *pissing me the fuck off!* And we can't even fireball the truck in case he's damaged in the crash!"

She pulled a hand from the wheel and smacked the side of her car. In the frenzy of her anger, she almost unleashed a blast of force while she was at it, but stopped herself. Roland had already mangled her ride enough.

"Yes," Aida added in a low voice. "He could at least be *gentle* with us."

Several more empowered stones flew at them from the rear of the truck, and Aida reached forward to deflect them, sending them shooting straight up into the sky. They cratered the earth somewhere behind them.

"*Yeah!*" Callie almost exploded. She was bleeding in four or five places after being tossed around the warehouse, and her jacket was pretty much ruined. "After this shit, *we* should be the ones fucking *him!* Who has a strap-on?"

If anyone did, Shannon thought, it would be Callie, but she didn't bother saying so aloud. Her focus was on the stupid redneck pickup truck that managed to stay slightly ahead of her. She could not decide whether she was more furious at Roland for continuing to evade her or at the little slut accompanying him for having lied to her on his behalf.

<hr>

Bailey, comfortable now that she was on a fairly straight and low-traffic stretch of road, waited for Gunney to pick up his phone. He answered after three rings.

"Bailey! You okay?"

"Yeah," she answered him, speaking quickly, "and we found the girls. Oberlin's gang took them and had them in a warehouse here in Portland. We're bringing 'em home. Somebody bake a cake and buy a thing of champagne."

"I knew you'd go after them," the old man stated. "And I figured you might even succeed. Listen, the sheriff is already up in Portland. The deputies are watching town while he calls in favors from people he knows in the city."

Bailey's heart quickened. That could be good, but it also might mean that the police were actively seeking them. She had no intention of calling the sheriff, though. That couldn't end well.

"Five or ten minutes before you called," Gunney went on, "they put out an APB and sent out the cavalry to look for that godawful Suburban and that swanky Jaguar. They're gonna find 'em and soon if they're still in Portland. Are they?"

Bailey cleared her throat. "They are," she said flatly. She filled him in on what had happened and asked him to let the sheriff know.

"Good. You need to get the hell away from them, then get out of Portland and come home. The cops will take care of the rest, you hear? I'll call the sheriff and tell him what you said. Just get everyone back safe."

"Well," she replied, "you're my boss, so I'll do what you say. Thanks for the update, Gunney, and make sure you give the new girl a proper lunch break. Over and out."

He half-snorted and half-chuckled. "See you soon."

Roland looked at her. "I heard that, but bad news. The terrible trio is gaining on us."

It was true; the silver car was now only about fifteen feet behind them. Bailey could see the witches staring at her with loathing.

And sirens were now audible—distant, but getting closer.

Bailey grunted. "We need to lose their asses right now. Do you think you could—"

She ran a yellow light as it turned red, and a school bus pulled out in front of her at a point where the road curved as it bore toward a freeway overpass.

"Oh, shit!" Bailey cried. She stamped on the brake and yanked on the wheel, swerving in time to avoid striking the bus but heading straight for a light post. She jerked the wheel back and they fishtailed, ending up half-on and half-off the road.

Roland clutched his seat and gritted his teeth, and the little girl between them, as well as the four in bed, screamed. The one in the back seat just covered her head.

Suddenly they were driving normally again, but they had another problem—Shannon had caught up. She pulled alongside them on the left.

"Hey!" the sorceress raged. "Pull over and let the inevitable happen, you stupid fucks!"

Roland pointedly avoided looking at her but scratched his nose with his middle finger.

"Yeah!" Callie added, once again contributing something classy and useful to the discussion. Aida just pouted at them.

Shannon honked and pulled farther ahead, trying to cut them off and forcing another car to pull onto the shoulder to avoid her. In the generalized clusterfuck, both vehicles were now driving only thirty miles per hour or so.

"Didn't you hear me?" the fuchsia-haired witch shrieked. "You dumb bitch!"

Bailey shot a hard glance at her. "Watch your language."

She jerked the steering wheel to the left.

Sparks flew as the Tundra smashed into and scraped the Jaguar, forcing it to drive on the shoulder, zigging and zagging as Shannon struggled to keep control. Then Bailey accelerated.

Roland looked at her bug-eyed. "Your truck," he marveled.

"Yeah, yeah, I can fix it later," she grumbled.

"Wait...*fuck*," the wizard added. "They're getting ready to throw some shit at us. I think we finally pissed them off enough to make them willing to use obvious magic in public. However..." he glanced around, "I have an idea."

The Jaguar started gaining on them again, and Bailey's spine went cold as she noticed all three of its passengers mouthing strange words in unison and raising their hands. Something crackled in the air.

Roland picked up the last piece of his rock collection, a jagged fragment about the size of a quarter. "Lean back, please," he told Bailey.

She had no idea what he was doing but obeyed, tilting her head and shoulders as far back as she could while maintaining control of the vehicle. Roland pitched the rock straight out the window...

Only for it to curve in midair and strike not the witches' car, but a fire hydrant in front of them. Loud pinging sounds split the air as the caps burst off, then a massive jet of foaming white water blasted into the Jaguar's interior.

"*Noooo!*" Shannon screamed, almost hysterical in defeat.

The artificial geyser stripped paint, killed visibility, and thrust enough kinetic energy against the car to force it to wobble straight into a dumpster, crunching the rest of the front end. The witches spilled out of the vehicle, along with the water that had flooded the interior.

Watching them in the rearview mirror, Bailey saw them thrashing around and raising their hands to claw at their faces. She didn't think it was because they were in pain, although the water was spraying pretty damn hard, but because it had completely destroyed their hairstyles, clothing, and makeup.

It almost looked like their faces were melting.

Roland lost it, abandoning all self-control as he flailed in his seat, heaving with laughter. "Oh, this is great. I wish I had that on video. That, *and* you sideswiping her precious car. Hah!"

Bailey, despite how seriously she'd been taking the whole pursuit, cracked up too. After the hell those three had put them through, it made her feel *quite* a bit better.

The sirens were still getting louder, though. Bailey picked up speed, but now that they no longer had to outrun anyone, she kept it within reason.

"Hey!" Roland exclaimed out of nowhere. "I was wondering. Back at the barn, you said something about your truck 'running rich' when Oberlin first showed up. I forgot 'til just now. What the hell does that mean?"

She was so annoyed she almost burst out laughing again. "Goddammit, Roland, now ain't the fuckin' time." She swerved around a taxi that was ambling along— looking for an address, probably.

Still, almost as soon as the words left her mouth, she found herself answering his question. After all, with so many people trying to kill them in the middle of a car chase, they might not get another chance to talk about trucks.

"Running rich," she explained, "is when a vehicle starts

burning excessive gasoline. It leads to that godawful stinky pungent gas smell you sometimes encounter on the highways, usually when people aren't keeping their vehicles properly maintained."

"Ohhh," Roland answered. "Interesting. You learn something new every day. Do you think this thing might be doing that right now? I thought I smelled something a minute ago."

She drew breath sharply over her teeth. "Not this lifted pickup truck, city boy. You're gonna pay for even insinuating that."

As he laughed, though, she wondered if he might be correct. She had been driving the Tundra awfully hard lately and hadn't had much time to check the engine.

Something tapped the rear window. It was Lauren, who seemed to have assumed leadership of the girls, knocking on it to get their attention.

Bailey locked eyes with her via the mirror. "Yes, honey?"

"Are we okay?" the girl asked. "Is it over?"

"Yes," Roland said. "For now."

Bailey nodded and repeated, "For now. You girls are safe, and we're headed home."

CHAPTER FIFTEEN

"He's dead," Shannon stated in a tone that might have frozen the sloshing puddles around them. "He's fucking dead. He is a fucking *homicide victim walking*, and he doesn't even realize it. So is his little whore of an alleged girlfriend."

She wiped her skin with a tissue, moaning in misery as she imagined having to talk to some mouth-breathing cop with her face streaked into oblivion and her hair a damp, tangled mess.

Aida frowned, her mouth looking like it was ready to drop off her face as she coiled her black hair and squeezed the water from it.

"He should at least be a sweetheart," she intoned, "and pay our expenses. I am sure we can *convince* him."

Callie tore off her jacket, which was now wrinkled with moisture in addition to being stained with blood and grime. She whipped it furiously against a small tree.

"Fuck that!" she snarled. "That son of a bitch. When we catch him, we're going to cut off his balls and *eat* them!"

Awkward silence set in.

"Um," Shannon riposted after a moment, planting a hand on her hip, "Caldoria, that was excessively gross and stupid. Way to try too hard. Besides, we *need* his balls. They have to remain intact, so we'll be nice and assume you're, like, speaking figuratively."

Callie pouted and looked away, making a "humph!" sound and crossing her arms.

"And," Aida added, "we will not murder him. It would be so much nicer to have him alive, only better—*persuaded* to give us the powerful children we want. But someone must pay for this."

Shannon glowered. The sirens were getting closer, but she could hide their tracks with a simple spell. They could abandon the vehicle and flee on foot. Despite the horrifying prospect that someone might mistake them for hookers, it would get them clear of the authorities. Then they could use a charm spell to ensnare a male motorist who stopped to help them since male motorists always stopped to help them.

"Yes," she confirmed, her voice low and hard. "Someone must pay, and she will. In addition to everything she did, we should also punish her for everything Roland has done while degrading himself in her presence."

Callie turned back, and her and Aida's eyes brightened.

"In fact," Shannon continued, her mood already improving, "we might be able to *convince* Roland to watch."

At long last, Agents Townsend and Spall were nearing the

end of the trail of devastation that had been wrought throughout northern and eastern Portland in the last two hours—the very visible and obvious devastation far too many people had witnessed.

Townsend straightened his tie. "Only three normies saw anything here. Nice simple operation, for once."

Spall adjusted his sunglasses. "Yes. Only mundane property damage, although it sounds like one of them might have seen the werewolves."

Both men frowned as they strode forth to do their duty.

They were almost indistinguishable from one another, and relatively average, nondescript men besides. Each was about six feet tall, medium build, white, stone-faced, clean-shaven, and with short hair of a dull brown. They wore matching dark gray-green suits that were almost black, but not quite.

Even after speaking to them for ten minutes, most people had difficulty recalling what they looked like.

One of the three "normies," an overweight guy with a red and flustered face, called to them. "Hey. Uh, officers? Christ, you guys are the feds, aren't you? Well, let me tell you what I saw. Might as well get it over with."

"Yes," said Townsend.

Spall motioned to the other two civilians, an old woman and a college-aged girl, whom the local police had already corralled and instructed to remain on the scene.

The three bystanders related their choppy, halting, half-assed account of what they'd seen, or thought they'd seen.

Someone throwing rocks out the back of a black truck. A white SUV with a tacky paint job and a travesty of a lift kit chasing them, then getting blasted off its wheels. Three party girls in a silver convertible of some sort picking up the chase and trying to force the truck off the road. The tubby guy claimed he saw something that looked like a giant dog or a panther or maybe a gorilla running alongside the road.

"Yes," said Spall.

Townsend held up a hand for the three witnesses to remain where they were, then turned to confer with his partner.

They mumbled nonsense words in slurred tones to one another, incomprehensible to anyone but them and a handful of their closest colleagues.

"Pretty standard," Townsend related. "The difficulty is a matter of quantity over quality. No one got a good look at anything."

"Affirmative," Spall responded. "But there are far too many people who got any look, even a brief, shitty one."

They turned back to the three witnesses in unison.

Townsend spoke first. "Thank you, good citizens, for your cooperation. The current investigation is sensitive and we can't talk about it, but we *can* tell you the matters we're dealing with should not be of any further concern to you."

Spall added, "It is unlikely you will be called upon to testify or anything like that. We and the local police have the situation well in hand."

The fat guy started to protest. "Okay, great," he huffed, "but how do you explain—"

Both agents whipped small sprayers out of their jackets, aimed, and fired. A mist of white gas shot into the faces of the three, causing them to stumble back, coughing. Then it was gone.

The gas had been designed for instant but short-term potency. A direct hit caused pronounced effects, but it dissipated within two seconds. That greatly reduced the danger to the agents.

As the citizens stood blinking in slack-jawed confusion, the agents repeated what they'd said a moment ago.

"What you saw here," Townsend added to the repeated information, "was the result of a gang war that spilled over into the streets. Normally such activities are confined to out-of-the-way places."

"Exactly," Spall affirmed. "This was a freak incident of professional criminals growing sloppy after a drug deal went awry. The principal offenders have either been apprehended or fled the state. You may return to your homes and rest well, knowing anything you saw here today was of no real concern."

The heavyset guy, the old lady, and the college girl nodded vaguely, their expressions blank. Then, stumbling as if in a dream, they departed.

After watching them leave, the nondescript but smartly-dressed duo turned in near-perfect synchrony and marched toward their car, which was parked a ways up the street where the Portland fuzz could watch it.

"Fuck," Townsend spat. "Goddamn idiot normies. It's always a shitshow cleaning up after the supernatural. Every asshole in America thinks he's an expert on something he half-saw once."

Spall snorted. "Yep. And the fucktard police vacillate between acting like they know what's going on and asking for bribes, or behaving exactly the same as the civvies, only they're better-armed and better-connected. What a bunch of dicks."

A kid playing with a half-deflated basketball watched them walk past, then shook his head. Lots of strange people in this neighborhood.

Townsend sighed. "Well, when it comes to conspiracy theories, at least a lot of people are dumb enough to believe in aliens."

As they came down the highway through the pass, the little town in the valley spread before them. At the edge of the built-up area, a bunch of cars had parked, and a crowd of people was standing around.

Roland put his feet up on the dashboard. "Oh, a festival. This ought to be fun."

Bailey squinted and leaned forward over the steering wheel. "The hell? There isn't a damn festival going on. More likely, it's…"

Her voice trailed off. She'd been about to say, "a lynch mob," but somehow she couldn't bring herself to speak the words. She could not accept that Greenhearth would allow it. Even if a gang of Weres had kidnapped children, the rest of the community here knew most werewolves did not do shit like that.

The black Tundra, banged up after its ordeal, rolled forward at a steady if chugging pace. The sun was almost down by now, but the streetlamps were on to compensate.

Bailey could identify the people milling around by the road.

Half were people she knew from Greenhearth. The other half was a mixed crew, but a few looked familiar—folks from nearby towns in the next valley or two up or down the mountain range, mostly Weres.

"Ohh." Bailey sighed, realizing at last what was going on. "Word must have spread that we, well, we have a delivery to make."

The girl sitting between them perked up. She was the smallest and youngest of the group, which was why the sedative had wiped her out to such an extent.

The five other girls sat up and looked around. Bailey pulled over and parked.

Someone in the crowd, a woman, cried out, "Oh, my God! She's safe!"

Then they were surrounded, and for three or four minutes, it was nothing but hugs and tears all around.

The parents embraced their daughters and checked to make sure they weren't hurt, saying loving words. The girls mostly cried. They weren't small children, but they'd been taken far, far out of their element, and now they were home.

Bailey and Roland sat in the truck just off the highway, unable to leave since the mob hadn't bothered to relocate yet. Somehow, their hands ended up entwined.

She smiled. "Well, Mr. Big Seattle Wizard, I think we did it."

"Oh, I know we did it," he replied, and something about the way he said the words made her blush. Fortunately, the interior of the truck was pretty dark. "We even survived. Not bad."

A short but solid figure wearing a baseball cap pushed through the mass of people. Bailey noticed him at once and waved him over.

"Hi, Gunney," she began. "This is Roland, by the way. How'd the new girl do?"

He was carrying a rag and wiping engine grease from his hands. "Howdy, Roland. And fine, mostly. Spilled a bit more oil than we'd like, and she could stand to get faster, but that's nothing experience won't fix. She ain't a fucking idiot, which always helps."

"Indeed." Bailey nodded. "Sounds like she's already better than Kevin."

He shrugged. "Time will tell. Anyhow, Sheriff Browne sends his regards and says thanks for the info. He'll be back ASAP. Has to clean up some red tape with the city folk since the PD up there managed to collect Dan Oberlin and his boys. Saw the cages and the warehouse, like you told him. Processing them as we speak, probably. You know how it is. How'd you like Portland?"

"Well, uh…" she began, searching for the right words.

Roland leaped to her rescue. "Oh, she did fine, aside from a bit of trouble with all the traffic. But that's to be expected."

Gunny nodded. "Fair enough. Anyway, looks like the welcoming committee wants to have words with you two, and they probably don't want my old grease-monkey ass in the way. I have to close up the shop for the night. You're working tomorrow, by the way, but we'll say afternoon shift. You probably need a good night's sleep."

"Yeah, yeah," Bailey riposted. "You know I'll be there."

He tilted his hat toward her and gave Roland a knowing glance, then turned and ambled off.

Bailey stepped out of the truck, suddenly wanting to stretch her legs and stand in the open air before the crowd pressed in. Roland did the same.

Then a bunch of parents, twelve in particular, formed a circle around them.

"Bailey," said Mr. Heuerman, "by all the gods! We can't thank you enough. You too, young man, whoever you are."

He smiled gently. Bailey thought he was doing rather well, faced as he was with twelve strange werewolves. "Roland, from Seattle."

The fathers each shook his hand, and everyone gave Bailey a hug.

Another man, one of the fellows from either the south side or one of the neighboring towns, remarked to Bailey, "So, I guess the rumors aren't true after all. About what sort of person you are—difficult and cantankerous and disrespectful and all that. Seems like your qualities haven't been fully recognized for almost, gosh, twenty-five years now."

Bailey smiled politely. "Thank you, sir. Rumors usually distort the facts one way or another."

Her muscles tensed when she realized what he'd meant —that she *was* good marriage material, someone they'd all want to introduce their sons to.

"See," the guy went on, "my boy, Derek...he's about your age, quite a bit older than Emma here," he ruffled his young daughter's hair, "he's getting to the point where he needs to think about, you know, settling down."

More men and women pressed in then, eager to join the conversation and offer their own suggestions about who Bailey should be talking to and associating with. A sinking feeling almost overwhelmed her, souring the good mood she'd been in just minutes ago.

Roland, standing a few feet off away, recognized her plight and stepped up to her side.

"Excuse me," he said, directing the comment mainly at Emma's father since he was still doing the bulk of the talking, "Mr...."

"Nimberger," he stated.

"Right, Mr. Nimberger," the wizard went on. "It's nice to talk to you all, but it's been a long day. So if I could just grab my girlfriend, we'll be on our way. I'll escort her home. I'm sure you can understand that I'm concerned about her getting some rest and privacy after everything that's happened."

The older man gaped wordlessly for a second as he stared at the couple, then he nodded. Everyone else shut up.

Bailey put her arm around Roland's waist, and he put his arm around her shoulder.

"Thanks, dear," she told him.

"Don't mention it," he replied.

Together, they strolled away from the crowd toward the higher ground to the northwest, where three tall figures—the Nordin brothers—stood and waved and waited. They'd come back for the truck. Then they were gone, vanishing from the sight of the group as dusk faded fully into night.

The cluster of parents milled closer together. All of

them were Weres, members of the Nordins' pack or of neighboring packs so closely aligned as to make little difference. They talked amongst themselves for a few minutes before they started to disperse for the evening. The sheriff's deputies had arrived to shoo them off anyway.

Three local moms had arranged themselves around a lamppost.

"Well," said one, "he's certainly handsome. And being from the big city and all, he's probably interesting and experienced."

"And sophisticated-like," another added. "Not used to people like us, and especially not Bailey."

The women tittered.

The third added her two cents in a lower voice than the other two. "He might be here today, but he'll be gone tomorrow. She'll drive him away, just like she does with every other outsider. And then, ladies? Well, it'll be time to introduce her to my boy Tommy."

They finally got settled at the Nordins' house, and everyone was asleep except Roland, tired as he was. He grabbed his phone from the recharger and brought up the arcane web, which was a corner of the dark web only available to magic users.

The whole WereWitch thing was bugging him because he'd noted several times when Bailey had reacted to his magic that couldn't be explained by her werewolf senses. He wasn't going to say anything since that could get her in trouble, but he wanted to know more.

Was she just a wolf who could sense magic, or was she one of the ruthlessly hunted WereWitches?

The End

You made it! Thank you so much for reading all the way to the end of this, my first book!

I grew up in Los Angeles and now live in a small town much like Bailey's in Oregon. It's only me, my cat Snowstorm, and my dog Josephine, who is a Labradoodle. Or something. I'm really not sure since she's a rescue, but that's as close as I can come. Did you ever wonder who rules the world? It's her (no, not the cat, thereby upending the myth that pervades the entire universe that felines are the superior life form). And from Oregon? Who knew?

The other day, Jo decided Storm was the devil's minion, and she must be eliminated. (Of course, it's entirely possible she's correct. We don't have sufficient evidence yet).

Me, I'm trying to write *Werewitch02*, so I only gradually become aware of the battle raging around me. It comes to a head when they simultaneously hit the LaZyBoy loveseat I write in and knock over my coffee. (Did I mention I live in a *small* town? No Starbucks, despite the law in the Pacific

Northwest that there be one on every street corner. I almost died before I got the Keurig with the Starbucks pods, and even now, it's not the same.) Coffee on my clean white t-shirt, coffee on Storm, and coffee on the navy-and-aqua blanket my Omi knitted me. Not a happy Writer! Who would have thought that a little of the manna from the gods could go such a long way?

Jo is miraculously unaffected. You'd think she planned it.

Storm, on the other hand, has the narrow-eyed look that suggests retribution (and her possible demonic origins that seemed to have been the root cause of the debacle).

Anyway, after much disagreement, both were relegated to the great outdoors—which will hopefully provide enough distraction to keep them uninjured. If I ever let them in again, everyone will need a bath, but that's another story.

Now that I mentioned Starbuck's, I may have to pop over to <redacted> to get one. Need me a cheese Danish too. And maybe some fish tacos.

I'm really hungry, so I'm going to wrap this up. It's readers like you who keep me going! Well, you and coffee. I hope you enjoyed Bailey's and Roland's first outing. Many more to come!

Until next time,
Renee

I COULDN'T DO THIS WITHOUT YOU!

With great appreciation to my beta readers
Larry Omans, Mary Morris, Kelly O'Donnell, John Ashmore, Dan Weigert

Thanks to my early readers, you rock!
Mary Morris ,Micky Cocker, Debi Sateren, Veronica, Stephan-Miller, James Caplan, Dave Hicks, Jackey, Hankard-Brodie, Kelly O'Donnell, Diane L. Smith, Dorothy Lloyd, John Raisor, Angel LaVey, Misty Roa, Peter Manis, John Ashmore, Deb Mader

Thanks to my editors

The SkyHunter Editing Team